LUKE'S K

Luke's fists clenched and opened again. His fingers tingled with the desire to reach out and touch the far horizon. Here they were destined to settle. Here they would bow to no one and pay tithes to no one.

'I'll make you a kingdom.' He spoke so softly that it might have been no more than a whisper of the mountain breeze. 'A kingdom fit for you, Jassy. All for you.'

JOHN BURKE

Luke's Kingdom

FONTANA / Collins

First published by Fontana Books 1976

Made and printed in Great Britain by
William Collins Sons & Co Ltd Glasgow

CHAPTER ONE

The boom of a signal gun bounced for an echoing moment between the two headlands. Pink and white parrots danced up like midges, squawking their indignation above the tangle of trees and shrubs, then swirled back among the olive-dark leaves. A ragged cheer answered them from the barque whose approach had been signalled by the cannon. People jostled up on deck, some gripping the handles of battered trunks as if prepared to heave them this very instant on to a quay which would miraculously thrust out from the crumbling cliffs.

'The new land,' said Jason Firbeck softly. 'A new beginning.'

He put his arm round his daughter's shoulders. His two sons braced their legs to the gentle sway of the deck – so different from the reelings and torments of these last thirteen weeks – watching the gap between the bluffs widen. A gleaming white lighthouse raised a welcoming finger on the southern side.

Jassy let her head sink against her father's arm. In spite of all the privations of the voyage she was somehow reluctant to leave the ship and set foot on firm land, to face whatever might lie in store for them. Instinctively she rubbed her cheek against his sleeve and turned her face towards the shimmering ocean, the vast expanse which lay between this coast and England.

He said: 'You're looking back.'

She tried to shake her head.

'See how Luke strains to be ashore. He finds the prospect entirely to his liking.'

'And you, father?'

His momentary hesitation made her want to weep for him, for herself, and for all that they had left behind.

'We shall see,' he said. 'Perhaps I'm too old for such adventure. Though age gives one more to forget.'

She knew he would never forget: never forget her dead mother, or the fields and moors of their own land. It was Luke who had urged them to break free, Luke who had spoken of new opportunity and a whole new life. Luke who believed that the riches of a new country could utterly wipe out the sad memories of the old.

Luke stood straight and tall, broad-shouldered and confident – straining to be ashore, as her father had said. Just once he glanced back at her and smiled. It was a reassuring but severe smile: it ordered her to be brave, to be as sure as he was of the future. Then his gaze was snatched away once more by the gateway through which they were sailing.

The open sea was banished. Jassy moved away from her father to lean on the rail, to see the landscape as Luke wished her to see it.

Certainly the banks of these sheltered waters were more appealing than the crumbling cliffs which faced the ocean. Stretches of white sand sparkled below tufts and swirls of greenery, tumbling down steep slopes and covering every ridge. Here and there a stream caught the light before disappearing into the secrecy of a shadowy cove.

Beside her a quiet voice said: 'So within the hour we shall be in Sydney Town.'

Jassy started. As she turned, the breeze caught her light brown hair and blew it across her eyes. She brushed it back; and the young man watched the movement of her arm with a yearning he could not hide.

'Mr Fogg,' she said. 'Yes, the town awaits us. The . . . the country awaits us.'

'I cannot view the future with anything but despondency. It will mean the parting of our ways.'

He had been a friend to all of them during the voyage. Except, possibly, to Luke. He had played cards with her father, listened to Samuel's vague plans for the estate they had not yet seen, and shown himself an especially attentive companion to Jassy. Occasionally she had observed Luke frowning, and once he had started to say something to her about keeping the fellow at arm's length; but she had cut him short. There were miseries and to spare during those interminable weeks. She would not have wished to be deprived of Aloysius Fogg's talk and kindness, the shyly flattering affection in his tone, so different from the raucous outbursts of those men who passed the time in gambling, boasting and quarrelling.

'We'll always remember you, Mr Fogg.'

'But it's not enough to be remembered.' Colour flooded into his pale cheeks, and his lips trembled. 'Miss Jassy, desperation forces me to speak. I do not want this voyage to end.'

She felt she ought to turn away and leave him. It was improper even to listen to the declarations which were trying to fight their way through his diffidence. But she found herself smiling.

'Are not fame and fortune awaiting you?' Lightly she tried to coax a responsive smile from him, recalling all that he had told them about his own future in New South Wales, setting up as a barrister in a country which most surely needed such young men.

'Empty things, Miss Jassy.'

His melancholy was not unlike her father's, but rather more dramatic.

'Empty?' she echoed. 'You must not think so.'

'Say we shall meet.'

It was easy enough to say, and in any case it was true.

Drawn together on the voyage, they could by now have been lifelong friends. And she would surely be glad of a friend in the alien places which lay ahead.

'I'm sure we shall.'

Samuel, older than Luke and more slow moving, more reserved in manner, had moved up towards the bows. Other passengers peered around obstructions and through sheets, trying to be sure. Was that not a church spire a few miles ahead?

Whitewashed walls began to break up the pattern of vegetation along the banks. A wisp of smoke curled up from a chimney. Two windmills stood like sentinels on a ridge. Brick and stone buildings clustered more thickly, shaping themselves into a township, as the barque swung in towards the main harbour. Some houses had trim verandas and little gardens enclosed by white palings. Others were little more than primitive, unadorned single-storey cottages. But the whole impression was one of such brightness that Jassy's heart lifted. The people who had built this place were, after all, people such as herself and her menfolk. This could be home for her, just as it already was for them.

On a fine morning in September, 1829, Jason Firbeck and his family set foot on the firm ground of Australia.

Thousands had come this way before them. Thousands had taken this same route; and not all of them willingly. Many a man had died at sea in chains, and many another had lived to regret not dying at sea. Pickpockets, forgers, highwaymen, Irish rebels, girls who had stolen a crust of bread or a lace handkerchief – they heard sentence pronounced, lay in the hulks and eventually set out bound and beaten like slaves, plagued by scurvy and foul sicknesses, to the southern continent. Soldiers were posted out to maintain order. Sheep were sent to stock the wastelands. And when the Government saw the dangers of founding a colony peopled mainly by convicts and ex-convicts, they decided to feed new, free settlers with land and promises. There was a need for squires and merchants; for a reliable new gentry in this unreliable new land.

Ambitious men and near-defeated men listened to the promises. Farmers harassed by bad crops, dwindling profits, and the arrogance of petty autocrats; soldiers cast off once their campaigns were ended and their country had no further need of them; hard workers and tricksters, idealists and bullies, men with Government grants of land and men escaping the law before that law transported them willy-nilly to this land in shackles: vessel after crowded vessel sailing through Port Jackson to Sydney brought a turbulent host of them. Each had his own ambition, or his own past failures to obliterate. There were those who asked only to be allowed to work, eat, and survive. And those who knew that wherever there were fellow human beings, there would be good pickings for predators. And those who saw themselves as conquerors.

Jason Firbeck, grey and gentle, a pious man who admitted to a life of disappointment but not defeat, envisaged an orderly life of honest labour building up an estate which would support his family and be handed on to them in due course. His older son, Samuel, had his father's features and much of his temperament: he was the methodical, the persevering one.

Luke, the younger, had inherited his mother's raven-dark hair and her wide, smouldering eyes. And on her death-bed he seemed to have snatched from her the torch of that angry energy which had worn her out and driven her to an early grave. It was their father who kept the official papers beside him, including the address of their lodgings in Sydney Town and the address to which they must head tomorrow. But it was Luke who knew each detail off by heart, and Luke who strode off to find an ox-dray for their luggage. Luke would make all the real decisions, as he had since he was a boy.

Jassy looked about her as she waited. In an unexpectedly smart shop-window, jewellery glinted. From another, a face grinned out at her: a dark, tattooed face. Above it a notice proclaimed: BAKED MAORI HEADS FRESH FROM NEW ZEALAND.

She gasped and turned away, only to be jolted by the sight of another dark brown face, grinning even more widely and vacantly. An aborigine sat in the gutter rocking to and fro and giggling hysterically. 'Me king. Me drunk pig king.' He sagged forward and retched, spat, and giggled again. Beyond him a gang of convicts, their legs chained together, shuffled and clanked across the street. On the far side of the street, more convicts in rags were digging what might be a drain: from the state of their sunken shoulders and scarred arms, it might as fittingly have been their grave. One without a tooth in his mouth looked up, then flinched and cowered down again as a guard raised the butt of his musket.

Jassy remembered the official promises – promises of a land in which reformed convicts were glad to act as servants, where men who had learned their lesson worked healthily in the fresh air and wandered freely and decorously about the townships.

'Come 'ere, me darlin'.' It took her a second to realize that the words had been addressed to her. 'Over 'ere, where I can reach you, eh?'

A grimed, squat man in the trench was leaning forward and staring at her with greedy, reddened eyes.

The redcoat took two steps along the edge of the trench and smashed his musket butt down. It cracked against the bone of the convict's left cheek. Blood spurted. The man crumpled.

'Work, you scum.'

The convict dragged himself up, clinging to the crumbling earth on the rim. His gaze found Jassy again. 'That was your fault, teasin' a man . . .'

Jassy let out a whimper of protest. Her father took her arm and led her round the heap of trunks and boxes.

'Hey, lads.' As she limped into the shelter of the baggage, her hip twisting as it always did when she tried to hurry, a derisive shout followed her. 'She's a cripple. But we ain't too partic'lar, eh? Hey! Hobble my way.'

There was the sound of another brutal crack, and a suppressed groan.

I shall hate this place, thought Jassy, shuddering. I knew we should be unhappy, I know I shall hate it, all of it. I know . . .

Luke was there. Luke, swinging down from the dray he had hired, with a quick smile for her which died abruptly into concern.

'What has upset you?'

Their father said: 'We must be on our way. This is no fit place to stand and chatter.'

Luke helped Jassy up so that she could sit at the front of the dray while the men loaded it. She tried to relax, not looking out from under the canopy at the sullen men working in the road, not daring to glance at another group which shuffled by, mumbling a dirge. Luke would protect her as he had always done. Born a cripple, she might never have walked if the little boy, so few years older than herself, had not patiently helped her, talked to her, embraced her when she cried, coaxed her into forgetfulness of pain. Without Luke there could have been no life for her; without him no future, perhaps, for any of them.

But there was no question of being without him. He was here, climbing up beside her, eager for them to be on the move.

Luke would see them to the promised land.

The road was long, straight and dusty. A fine black sand blew across the plain and eddied around the oxen as they trudged on. Jason drove the first wagon, with Samuel walking beside the animals. It had taken a lot of time in Sydney Town, a lot of bargaining and a lot of their small capital, to acquire provisions and transport. Jassy was happy to have the reins of the smaller horse-wagon in her hands; glad to have something to do, to feel them plodding onwards, drawing imperceptibly closer to that smoky range of blue mountains.

Luke rode ahead, leading the way.

They passed a few medium-sized farms and then began to cross a lumpy desert of stone and parched grass hummocks. Bushes smeared the landscape ahead like a scattering of dark smuts.

On one tiny knoll stood a tottering bark hut which looked as if it would not withstand the first high wind. A few goats were tethered near by, and pigs rooted in a patch of clumsily fenced ground. A man stooping over what might have been a vegetable plot straightened up to watch them go; but did not so much as raise his hand to answer her friendly salute.

Beyond the mountains things must be better. Beyond the mountains, their official concession must be quite different from this unrewarding plain.

Luke's voice drifted back. He stood up in his stirrups, waving the two wagons to slow down.

They came to a halt. By the roadside was a weather-boarded shanty inn, with a large adjoining paddock. Two men and a woman were dragging hurdles across the road to divert a jostling, bleating flocks of sheep off the track and into the enclosure.

Jassy edged to one side of the hard seat to get a better view.

'Where did you find 'em?' one man asked as the animals stumbled through.

'Feller gone bust up Potter's Creek. Traded him a horse for the flock.'

'Mm. Good fleece on 'em.'

'Shilling a pound that wool could fetch in Sydney. That and the meat – make me a two-horse man, I reckon, an' a bit over.'

Luke closed in on the men and leaned down to speak to the fatter of the two. There was a shrug, a laugh, and an expansive gesture towards the inn.

Fifteen minutes later the wagons were off the road, the animals tethered and feeding on the spiky grass, and Jassy was contemplating a lump of meat on a plate set in front of her, and a lump of something else – a sort of thick round cake as speckled and gritty as the landscape.

'Don't know what that is, dear?' The innkeeper's wife, a massive woman in a loose cotton smock stained with mutton fat, treated herself to a hoarse chuckle. 'It's plain you're fresh off the boat.'

'It looks very good,' said Jason dubiously, settling himself on the bench beside his daughter.

'Damper, that is. Damper and mutton – you won't come to much harm on that.'

'Damper?'

'Good wholesome flour and water, and a bit o' salt to taste. Cook it in the ashes, we do. If you'd fancy some for pudding, we can pour a bit of tea and sugar on.'

'Thank you. I think this will suffice.'

The tap-room filled up as afternoon shaded into evening. Two more travellers arrived, and the men of the neighbourhood came in two or three at a time and settled down to some steady drinking. All of them smoked short dudeen pipes, and most of them kept their hats on – woollen caps, tanned skins of unidentifiable animals, and a few battered straw hats fraying away at the brim.

Luke sauntered away from the family and sat beside the man who had driven his flock into the paddock. Jason watched uneasily.

Luke said: 'How much do you want for your sheep?'

'You lookin' for a flock, mister?'

'If the price is right.'

'I can see' – the tallow lantern struck a glow of cunning from the man's eyes – 'you're a man of means.'

The landlord of the inn snorted. 'We 'ad a man o' means stop last night. Real gentleman, I'd 'a thought. Till I ups this morning to find him flitted. Not a penny. Food, lodging grog . . . nothin'.'

Jason moved towards the group. 'We are not without resources.'

'Which we propose to keep,' said Luke brusquely. 'Leave this to me, father.'

'You know nothing of business. I shall attend to it.'

'Father . . .'

But Jason Firbeck was not going to allow his son to override him. Jassy's heart sank. Her father had made mistakes and taken wrong decisions before – 'Ruined us,' Luke had bitterly said when the end came and they decided Australia was the only answer. Seeing Luke's mounting passion now, she wished their father could have stood aside and let Luke have his way.

A griping pang wrenched her stomach. She could not suppress the instinctive movement, clutching herself and trying to sit upright.

Luke was at her side immediately. 'Your stomach?'

'The same as on the ship. I'm sorry. I – '

'I doubt there's anywhere in this hovel.' He surveyed the tap-room. Silently she implored him not to ask the obvious question, not to invite the guffaws of the drunkards and the harridan who swaggered among them. 'You'll have to go in the bushes,' he murmured.

She thought of the darkness on scrub and sand, of unknown animals which might lurk in the mysterious night. Sensing her fears, Luke took her by the hand. A few heads turned as they left the bar, but Luke's expression forbade them to snigger or risk even one word.

'Come on,' he said, close to her ear. 'Come with big brother.'

'No, I – '

'Come and look at the stars.'

By the time they got back their father had concluded his deal. Proudly he told them the terms. Luke's mouth tightened, and his knuckles thrust up white beneath the flesh.

In the morning, as they set out again, he reined back to ride for a while beside Jassy. Words snapped out of him like chewed tobacco. She had the impression that he had been awake all night, calculating and cursing to himself.

'We saved that man two days' travel to Sydney. Did father take that into account?'

'I'm sure he did what he thought fair.'

'Fair? We should have shorn them, left him the fleeces, and taken the sheep for nothing. Now we carry the full weight across the mountains.'

The mountains . . . closer now, yet still hazy and remote. They formed a barrier between the coastal settlements and the uncharted interior, a jagged arc which had taken years to penetrate. In the early years there had been enough land, even with the sandy stretches and the unpredictably flooding river flats, to maintain the colonists spreading thirty and forty miles out of Sydney harbour. But the greater challenge and the greater rewards must surely lie beyond.

The peaks beckoned the Firbecks, as they had beckoned

and tantalized others until a way through the barrier was won. Somewhere beyond they could slow, and stop, and settle.

At the Parramatta toll-gate six or seven men and a dejected woman sprawled at the roadside. As the oxen lumbered to a standstill, one of the men got to his feet. He must have been about thirty years of age, with a disillusioned but insolent gaze. It settled on Jassy and at once dismissed her. For him, the older man of the party was the one who counted. He waited for Jason to approach the lounging group, with Samuel at his elbow.

From where she sat Jassy recognized affectionately the awkwardness of her father's attempt to sound both courteous and commanding.

'You're offering yourselves for work?'

There were a few pessimistic nods. The man standing erect did not go even to that length. He simply waited.

'My name's Firbeck,' said Jason. 'First Lieutenant, Royal Navy, retired. Believe in discipline. Hard work but decent conditions. Convicts, were you?'

Their dour expressions gave him his answer.

'Ticket-of-leave men? Let's have a look at you.'

The queasiness in Jassy's stomach had nothing to do with the lingering shipboard sickness. It was a sour awareness of the contrast between what they had been told in England and what they now saw. These were the freed and penitent felons who were eager to help in the building of a new society. As they scrambled to their feet there was no resentment in their manner; but no eagerness, either. Only resignation.

'I have land here,' said Jason proudly, 'granted by the Government in England. I'm looking for an overseer and a shepherd.' He reached the man who had been first up, silently waiting. 'Your name?'

'Charlton.' The reply was as cool as the man's sardonic

eyes. 'Overseer.' The contemptuous gaze raked the flock of sheep milling around the wagons. Luke was trying to keep them under control. Charlton said: 'That lot came from Potter's Creek. I'd know them anywyere.'

'Correct,' said Jason.

'You'd have done better selling the fleeces. They'll be ruined in the rivers on your way.'

Luke glanced at Jassy. Their father hurried along the line of men. The woman half raised her hand, then let it drop. She saw that with a young daughter there he needed no female servant.

'What's your name?' It was addressed to a sturdy, gap-toothed older man at the end of the line.

'Shepherd.'

'Not what you do. I asked – '

'Both, sir. I'm Shepherd the shepherd.'

'He works with me,' said Charlton.

'Very well. Stand over. The rest of you – I'm sorry, but we need no more.'

They were used to slights, to dismissal, to far worse. The only one who appeared different from his companions was a younger man who, Jassy now realized, had not even risen to his feet in the first place. He sat close to a tethered horse, some distance from the others, his chin on his knees. There was something about the set of his head which she found familiar.

'Father!' It was torn from her.

Jason followed the direction of her incredulous gaze.

'Mr Fogg?' He was as amazed as Jassy.

Aloysius Fogg got slowly to his feet at last. 'Mr Firbeck. Samuel.' He raised his dark black hat, so formal and so incongruous in this setting. 'Miss Firbeck.'

'*You* surely do not seek employment?' said Jason.

'I . . . I am on my way to Bathurst. I've been offered a Government post there.'

'Ah. A legal position.'

'I . . . er . . . no, not exactly. I wonder, if we are travelling the same road . . . perhaps I might accompany you?'

Jassy willed him to look at her. He turned and smiled, with a shamefaced sadness she could not fathom.

Her father said: 'Now. Charlton, Shepherd. As to your wages. Twelve shillings all found, rations – '

'Ten,' said Luke loudly and firmly.

'My boy, if you're presuming to – '

'Ten shillings. That's the going rate.'

'I'm not greedy.' Charlton was quick to decide where the authority lay. 'Ten it shall be.'

Aloysius Fogg freed the rein of his mount, a tired bony, broken-down specimen, and made his way towards the horse-wagon. Jassy's heart was fluttering. She was sure it was all too obvious, but did not dare put her hand to her breast to calm it

'So you're travelling with us.'

'I trust it pleases you. What I've done,' the young man blurted out, 'I've done for you.'

'For me?'

'I have changed the course of my life.'

'I don't understand.'

He said: 'I love you.'

The road degenerated into little better than a mud track, then hardened into perilous ruts. Their pace was so slow that Jassy saw her father near to despair, Luke on the brink of a mighty rage. If it had been left to her father, or even to Samuel, they might have turned back, though none of the places they had left behind offered any comfort. At an inn and again at a tumbledown store they had been told how lucky they were to be travelling at this time. There had been a drought, and water was scarce; but if there had been rain, then the roads would by now be impassable and the rivers would have overflowed their banks.

They came to a river. It took all of a day to make a raft of logs to ferry sheep and wagons across. Chairs fell in the water; a dozen sheep were lost. But this kind of challenge invigorated Luke. His anger turned to exuberance. First the river, then the lower slopes of the Blue Mountains, then the tortuous defiles and dizzy canyons of the mountains themselves. The rocky pinnacles were no longer blue, but red. Cliffs of orange sandstone fell away into gorges blue with a eucalyptus mist, and long slopes of fallen rubble plunged into the thick carpet of trees. The oxen stumbled as they hauled the heavy dray over one ridge, only to find another beyond it. At places Charlton, Shepherd and Samuel had to go ahead and manhandle boulders out of the way. Luke shouted at his brother and the two hired men, cursed the beasts, and drove them on; and sang interminably, exultantly to himself. They stared from one steep wave crest to another, some capped with white breakers of dead wood above the green and blue troughs of the canyons.

Until, at last, there were no farther peaks and no more splintered ridges ahead. Only a dizzying fall, an ebb of trees into the vast swell of a far-reaching, mauve and brown and olive landscape, rolling and tilting away as far as the eye could see. The track they were following plunged and was lost in it, a mere ripple gathered into a pulsating sea.

Jassy stood beside Luke. She knew what he had longed for, and saw through his eyes what he now saw. Below them lay their new homeland, free from the oppressions and snobberies and deprivations of the old. Luke's fists clenched and opened again. His fingers tingled with the desire to reach out and touch the far horizon. Here they were destined to settle. Here they would bow to no one and pay tithes to no one.

'I'll make you a kingdom.' He spoke so softly that it might have been no more than a whisper of the mountain breeze. 'A kingdom fit for you, Jassy. All for you.'

CHAPTER TWO

Between the spokes of the dray wheel Jassy saw the comforting silhouettes of the men against the leaping fire. Somewhere a bird with a rasping call chattered to itself, then subsided. The sheep bleated and fidgeted; but they, too, were tired. Peace descended on the mountainside. She tugged the blanket up to her chin, turned over for the tenth time, and waited for sleep to come. It was so much better out in the open than it had been in the shabby inns they had risked a couple of nights on their journey. Yet she was wakeful, sure she had been bitten by some insect in the leg and neck, unsure of things which might creep from the red sandstone crevices.

'Miss Jassy.'

The murmur of her name jerked her half upright. The blanket fell away from her throat, where she had undone two top buttons, the better to breathe.

Aloysius Fogg was a dark shape, blotting out the fire and her father and brothers around it. He wriggled under the wagon and slid alongside her.

'Mr Fogg, please . . .'

'Jassy, I need you.'

A brighter glow from the fire flushed his face. His hand reached for the third button on her dress and flicked it loose.

'Please.' The cry was wrenched from her.

Fogg pulled away. At the fire, Jason hunched round to peer into the uncertain shadows.

'Jassy? Did you call?'

There was a tense silence. Then Jassy replied: 'I'm all right, father.'

Fogg's hand groped back. 'Bless you.' His fingers tightened insistently on her breast. 'I need you. I – '

'Leave me,' she said in a fierce undertone. 'Leave me alone.'

'I can't. My dearest, Jassy, don't you understand, won't you – '

'Do you wish me to call?'

Defeated, his hand dropped away from the swell of her dress. She heard him sigh, and had to conquer a shameful impulse to draw him close and console not only him but the tremors within her own body.

After he had crawled away she lay awake until the fire had died away into embers. Her father, Luke and Samuel settled down for the night. Where Fogg had finally chosen to bed down, she did not know. She was sure he would not return to her.

At last she slept.

In the morning a mist drifted from the gullies and softened the harsh redness of slope and crag. It was cold but beautiful. She felt that the sun would soon draw the mist away like a curtain, to reveal undreamt-of splendours.

Her father was shaving, dipping his brush into a tin mug standing on an up-ended box. He was not the earliest riser, though. Fully dressed and carrying his valise, Aloysius Fogg picked his way over the loose shale and spoke to him. Jason's razor remained poised in mid-air. He looked bewildered.

Then Fogg approached Jassy.

She stiffened, ready to counter whatever he might dare to say to her.

'I have come to say goodbye.'

It took her unawares. 'Goodbye?'

'I think I should proceed independently. I must tell you – my madness has left me.'

Again she felt that deplorable weakness, her mind sternly rejecting him while her flesh tingled with a consciousness she dared not admit. 'I will not think of it again,' she said. 'I would not wish you to – '

'Please, Miss Jassy. I've learned my speech. Let me deliver it.' He stood almost to attention. 'I never was a barrister. I couldn't pass the examinations. My uncle tired of me, sent me here. Unhappily the letters of credit he provided were useless. The man for whom I was to clerk had lost all his money, together with such as he was holding on my behalf.' Jassy put out her hand, but he would not touch it. Doggedly he concluded: 'My friendship with this family has been the most precious association of my life. Now I must seek my own salvation. I hope you can remember me as . . . some sort of gentleman.'

'Indeed we can, Mr Fogg.' Jason stood beside Jassy, dabbing his face dry. 'Nor ever doubted it.'

As the young man rode away, Luke let out a mocking whistle. 'Well, well, well.' He joined the others. 'It's my belief that the *gentleman* who flitted from that inn, that place the other side of Parramatta, without paying, must be none other than – '

'Luke! I will not allow it. Not if you speak the unworthy slander which I fancy is in your mind.'

Father and son confronted each other. At last Luke raised one unrepentant eyebrow and turned away.

As if Fogg's departure had been the signal for their own, Jason began to rumble orders and pace to and fro.

The mist was dissolving into transparent wisps as they began the descent. Colour flooded slowly into the landscape, outlines sharpened, the distance grew vaster.

'Our paltry fifty sheep,' growled Luke. 'We should have had five thousand.'

On the level they came to a meandering stream. Luke and Samuel plunged in and washed away the dust and sweat of the mountain crossing, laughing and splashing like a couple of boys. Which, thought Jassy with sudden, womanish remoteness, was just about what they were. She hoped – and there was an inexplicable anguish in the hope – that Luke would be able to laugh more and not have to carry too much on his shoulders. They had known few of the pleasures of youth in their own country. Here there must somehow be time for such things – else why had they come?

Another day of slow progress, with Charlton and Shepherd marshalling the sheep, chivvying them, keeping the little procession moving.

And another night by the fire, this time out on the plain, sheltered only by a clump of withered, prematurely gnarled blue-gum trees.

Samuel squatted near the crackling wood and leaned forward to open a book, tilting the pages towards Jassy in the spurts of flame.

'This is the only one I can find. The trunk with the rest of your books must be underneath.'

'Which is it?'

'Shelley. And I know your favourite poem.'

He was an awkward reader, without much expression, and the sonnet did not mean to him what it did to her. But she loved the earnest sound of his voice and his tenderness.

Luke listened for a few seconds, then got up. He could never settle to a book, a poem, a tale by the fireside. He was forever restless – wanting her to have the best of everything, yet suspicious of all that was not connected with work and security and more work.

From the corner of her eye she noticed her father talking to Charlton. The man's demeanour was brash and offhand He had shown himself indifferent to all of them as they travelled, other than Luke. And even with Luke he had difficulty keeping the lounging insolence out of his manner. Now he nodded at Jason, shrugged, and gestured off into the darkness of the land they must still traverse. He seemed to be laying down some ideas of his own.

In the morning he set out ahead, riding fast, released from the stupidity of the slow-moving, intransigent sheep.

'Eighteen hours,' said Luke. 'He's been gone eighteen hours.'

The wagons creaked on their way, Shepherd and his dogs kept up a continual dance to urge the sheep along. Samuel and Jason led the oxen, their hands and shoulders and eyebrows grey and pink with dust.

Luke rode up parallel with his father, who tried to sound confident.

'He'll be waiting for us on our land.'

'Can't see why you had to send him on ahead.'

'He knows this territory. Knows where our stretch is – over that ridge, he said it'd be. And he can size up the dispositions, save us time setting up camp.'

'It was his idea?'

'We talked it over.'

'Mm,' said Luke. 'Yes.'

He spurred his horse off the track towards the low, undulating ridge which curved in from the north-west. A short scramble and they were at the top. His father came away from the wagon and followed more slowly.

The rolling countryside spread richly away below them. It was all a man could desire. But there was something disturbing about it. Somehow they must have miscalculated; must have got distance or direction wrong.

'Excellent pasture,' breathed Jason. 'Far grander than I would have believed.'

'This land,' said Luke flatly, 'has all been cleared.'

'What do you mean?'

'See for yourself. Cleared. 'Of it's timber.' Luke surveyed a thicket of tree stumps in the near distance, some burnt to ash, some still jutting up raw from the earth.

'Lord Brisbane would hardly have granted me land already committed to somebody else. Fetch the sextant. We can soon tell whether this is ours or not.'

Luke rode back to find the brass-bound case and bring it to the ridge. Lifting it gently down from the saddle, he set it on a flat-topped stone and opened the lid.

The case was empty.

Jason stared, speechless. Luke slammed the lid shut and turned towards the wagons again.

'Shep!'

'Aye, sir?'

Luke strode down the slope. 'Where did Charlton go?'

'Go? I thought him and Mr Firbeck settled for him to ride on afore us and – '

'Where did he really go?'

Shepherd shook his head. Then shook it again, doubling up as Luke punched him hard in the belly.

'What d'you think you're doing?' shouted Jason.

'How much has Charlton taken?' As Shep tried to straighten up, Luke swung another vicious punch. 'And *where is he?*'

'Gone, mister.' The words screeched hoarsely out.

'You mean run off?' Jason reached them. 'With my sextant?'

Luke sprang into the wagon. He rummaged through the boxes, tore open a lid; and swore. Tea, sugar, tobacco – as much as one man could carry. And Jassy's books.

He towered above the gasping Shep. 'Books,' he raged. 'What would a creature like that do with books?'

'Sell 'em, mister.'

Jason said: 'But he couldn't have carried all that lot away without our noticing.'

'Those damn inns we stayed at,' said Luke. 'A bit at a time, that's how he did it.'

'Not the sextant,' said Shep.

'You mean he didn't tell you about the sextant? He kept that for himself.'

'Not him. Not what I meant at all, mister.'

This time Luke hit him full in the face. Jassy whimpered a protest.

'Why didn't he take you?' Luke demanded.

'I've had enough.'

'Enough what?'

'Running.' Shep smeared the back of his hand across blood and tears. 'I wanted to stay with you. That's the truth, I swear it.'

'Where's he gone?'

'Likely the village. Twenty-thirty miles on, over that way. That's all I'd guess.'

Luke snapped open the box under the driver's seat. At least Charlton had left them their pistols. He took one out and reached in for ammunition.

Jason said: 'I forbid the use of firearms.'

Tight-lipped, Luke ignored him. Riding off into the unknown, he had no intention of leaving himself defenceless.

The village boasted the name of Kinbone. And also boasted a barracks, the only building of any substance in the place. There was a timber-framed store, and facing it a shanty inn with an extension at the rear, tacked on and roofed at some eccentric angles. Chickens pecked to and fro. Processions of sheep had fouled the street and alleys. The reek of their droppings, with which Luke was already becoming familiar, was more concentrated here than out on the open country. Convicts plodded unnoticing through the mess, enviously glancing at the open door of the inn, though its name offered them little solace: *The Trooper's Rest.*

Luke stamped into the tap-room.

A young woman sweeping the floor let herself come to a halt a few feet away from him. She was a lean, dark thing with a tangle of black hair and a slack, inviting mouth. 'I'm

Rosie.' She rubbed her left hand over one out-thrust hip.

'Where's the landlord?'

'I'll fetch her.'

A woman's voice rose in a shriek of rage, unmuffled by the wooden walls and a couple of closed doors.

'Not another night. Not one more day, d'ye hear?'

'Madam, I implore you – '

'Cheating a poor woman out of an honest penny. Out, d'ye hear me, before I fetch a soldier to give you board and lodgin' you won't have to pay for.'

'Madam, will you not understand? My funds have been delayed. Any day they will arrive, and you'll be paid in full.'

Luke recognized the voice. He edged past Rosie and out on to the rickety veranda, making his way to the corner of the building.

'And when they do arrive' – the woman was short but plump and full-bosomed, with tight fair curls, a drink-blotched face, and a rasping voice jagged enough to have sawn the original timbers of this tavern – 'you shall have me finest room. With Rosie for company . . . if you've got the strength.'

Luke said: 'I have brought Mr Fogg's money.'

At once the woman was all smiles. Hearing the unexpected voice, Fogg dodged past her. There was a tic of apprehension in his cheek, but he thrust out his hand, even more effusive than the harridan was now trying to be.

'My dear Luke. Goodness me, that was close.'

'How much does he owe?' Luke did not take his eyes off the young man.

'Eleven shillings, eight pence. It's a good room, sir. One o' my best. Only the very best for a real gentleman, here.'

'Presently.' Luke took Fogg's arm. 'Come along. We have business.'

'Daylight robbery.' Fogg chattered as they went into a

dingy room at the side of the building. 'The blankets crawl – ticks, roaches – I'm all but eaten . . .'

Luke released him, saw the valise, threw it on the bed and opened it. The sextant lay on a folded shirt.

'I – you must understand – I intended to return it.'

'Because nobody would buy it?'

'No. Certainly not.'

Luke swung and hit Fogg hard, enjoying the pain in his own knuckles, hitting harder than he had hit Shep because there was more reason for it. Fogg went down and stayed down. Only his head tilted fearfully up.

'Did you tell . . . the others . . . about this?'

'No.'

'I couldn't help it. I don't know what it is, I've always been . . . when I was a boy, my tutor, my mother . . .' He fumbled breathlessly for words. 'I thought perhaps if I could start again out here, if Jassy loved me, if – '

'She doesn't.'

Fogg gulped. 'What are you going to do?'

'I want Charlton.'

'What has he to do with it?'

'He stole my sister's books. Books she loved. They were everything to her.'

Fogg stole a dubiously hopeful glance at him. He was eager to transfer the blame and the vengeance.

'He was here. I heard him.'

'When?'

'Today. With that dreadful . . . that woman.'

'Stay here.'

Luke went down a stale-smelling passage into the bar. The woman smirked invitingly and spread her hands to offer him the room, herself, the array of bottles and stone jars unevenly arranged along a shelf.

'Never got properly introduced, did we?' she said archly. 'Moll, that's me. Had a surname once. Him across the way.'

She waved towards the door, and the store on the other side of the street. 'But don't give that a thought, because you don't catch *me* givin' it a thought after all this – '

'I'm looking for Charlton,' said Luke curtly.

'Who?'

'Charlton.'

'Can't say I know him.'

Luke laid a neat pile of eleven shillings and eight pennies on the counter. As she reached for it, he covered it with his hand.

Moll glowered. 'This man you're talking about – why d'you want him?'

'My father engaged him as an overseer.'

'And he made off with your provisions.' When Luke nodded, she chuckled and shook her head in exaggerated disapproval. 'It's a bad habit. God knows I've told him.'

'And my sister's books,' said Luke with deadly calm. 'And a sextant.'

'He's going up in the world.'

'It's valuable.'

'He can't even read.'

'I'm talking about the sextant.'

But he wasn't. Not really. And he knew it. He was talking about Jassy and her books, the books they had made room for when so many other things had had to be sold off or left behind: his sister's treasures.

'If you're thinking of handing him over,' said Moll, 'it'll mean a hundred lashes.'

'When's he coming back?'

'If we split on him, he'd tear us apart.' As Luke began pocketing his money again, she spat out: 'Oh, he comes for Rosie.'

Luke took out a coin and held it up. Rosie moved from a corner of the room towards it.

He said: 'When's Charlton coming back?'

'He'll beat me, sure as – '

'So will I.'

'I think you would, too,' said Moll admiringly.

'It's either Charlton or Rosie. *You*, Rosie. Take your pick.'

'You'd . . . you'd be sure and get him?'

'Quite sure.'

Moll said: 'Oh, for God's sake, tell 'im.'

'He's coming this evening,' said Rosie shakily.

Luke let the coin drop into her outstretched hand, and once more counted out the money for Fogg's room. This time he let Moll scoop it up.

'Now,' he said: 'which way will he come?'

The setting sun touched flame to the sky and tinged a few shreds of cloud with scarlet. Trees became black skeletons against the blaze. The gap in the rocks through which the trail led was sharp-edged and limned with the same iridescence.

Fogg swallowed unhappily. 'I don't care for this. I am not cut out for a highwayman.'

'Quiet.'

Luke slipped the catch on his pistol and propped himself against a massive boulder. Several times he had thought to catch the faint clip-clop of hoofs. Now, straining forward, he was sure.

'I'd give my right arm not to be here,' lamented Fogg.

'Shhh!'

A man on horseback was framed in the opening. He came on at a leisurely pace. A kookaburra let out its eldritch call. Fogg started, his foot scrabbling against some shards of rock. The rider turned his head. The profile against the sunset was, beyond doubt, Charlton's.

Luke stepped out and seized the horse's bridle.

'You're under arrest.'

'What the hell . . .'

Charlton tried to knee his horse on, but Fogg blundered forward and grabbed the nearer stirrup. Luke got his arm beneath Charlton's leg and heaved. The man came out of the saddle and thumped to the ground.

'Take his gun,' Luke snapped.

Gingerly Fogg groped for Charlton's pistol.

'What's this about?' Charlton was getting his wind back.

'You know very well. On your feet.'

Charlton got up, making a shot at his old arrogance. 'What you hoping to prove, cully?'

'There's a little matter of food and tobacco and – '

'You lost some rations crossing the river? Come to that, you never had enough in the first place. Nothing to do with me, not that I can see.'

'Save your breath. You'll need it to explain to the military.'

'Christ, you'd not . . .'

Luke prodded Charlton with his pistol. After a moment's hesitation the man started walking. Fogg brought up the rear with the sextant under his arm.

There were lights in the barracks, and a guard at the rear of a convict chain-gang held a sputtering torch high above his head. Luke nudged Charlton on so that they could take advantage of the flare to see where they were going. They followed the convicts through the gates and up to the guardroom door.

In the lamplit office a young lieutenant with chubby features and blue, tired eyes was shaking his head despondently over a map. He looked up with something almost like a welcome in his face as a sergeant marched in with the three newcomers. Whatever might be going on, it would break the monotony.

'Charlton!'

'You know this man,' said Luke without surprise.

'We know him, yes.'

Luke took the sextant from Fogg and laid it on the desk. 'He stole this from my father.'

The lieutenant frowned. 'Charlton? Not like him. Usually supplies, provisions, trinkets – things he can sell so we never find anything on him to prove it. But a sextant!' He glanced dubiously at his sergeant. 'Where would he hope to sell that?'

'Couldn't say, sir.'

'Nevertheless,' said Luke, 'he stole it.'

'It's a lie,' said Charlton. 'And you know it's a lie. You're trying to get me on that because you know you couldn't get me on – '

'You caught him with it in his possession?' asked the lieutenant.

'Yes,' said Luke.

'I see.' The officer turned the sextant under the light to read the inscription. 'Firbeck, J. Eighteen hundred and ten. Your father, you said?'

'Jason Firbeck, yes.'

'Why would he use this?'

'He's a retired naval officer.'

The lieutenant thawed slightly. 'I'm Robarts. Lieutenant Robarts, commander of this . . . this post.' They shook hands. Charlton's mouth twisted sourly in defeat. 'We'll need to prepare a charge document for you to sign. While we're waiting, perhaps you'll join me in a drink.'

It was dark when they returned to the inn. News had travelled ahead of them. Moll was waiting on the veranda, her arms folded across her breasts, smoking a short meerschaum pipe. She spat on the ground as Luke approached.

'You rotten shit.'

He walked past her. She hurried in, brushing past Fogg in her haste to get to the bar and pour drinks. When Luke gestured that she should have one herself, she slopped spirit into a tumbler and raised it with a mixture of awe and revulsion.

'Charlton never stole that sextant. He's not that daft. It was your friend.' She nodded as Fogg choked on his drink. 'I saw it in his room that afternoon. Accidentally, o' course. When we was cleaning.'

Before Fogg could stammer out a denial, Luke said: 'Who'll believe you? Your word against a gentleman's.'

'You catch on quick, don't you? One law for the nobs – '

'And one for the scum. Like Charlton.'

'You know they'll flog him.'

'I wanted to be sure of that. And' – Luke nodded at Aloysius Fogg – 'he shall hear it.'

Fogg went pale; tried to speak; then saw the full withering contempt in Luke's eyes and reaching for his glass again, drank shudderingly deep.

Justice was swift out here. As soon as the sun was up and blazing on the barrack square, Charlton was led out. Stripped to the waist, he was pushed forward and strapped to the punishment triangle. Luke stood on the veranda to watch the preparations. When he saw the doctor and the scourger appear, he called over his shoulder:

'Tell Fogg I want him.'

Rosie hurried indoors. Moll stood for a moment beside Luke, weighing him up.

He looked out beyond the end of the sordid village street, out to the rolling wilderness which lost itself in dust and woodland and scrub and sky.

'Whose land is that?'

'That?' Moll snorted. 'No one's. Blacks. Squatters. Runaways.'

'Squatters?'

'They just take the land. Don't wait for a by-your-leave. Farm it the way it suits 'em. Who's to argue?'

Fogg cringed out on to the veranda. He was in time to see the doctor stoop over Charlton, stretched out on the triangle, and peer round into his face. A nod of approval, and the scourger braced himself in position.

'One,' cried the sergeant.

Clear and crisp in the morning air came the crack of the lash across human flesh. It struck a moan from Fogg. Nothing from Charlton.

'Two,' cried the sergeant. The slash of the impact, and this time a thin howl of agony, twisting an echo from Fogg.

'I would give my right arm to – '

'So you said before.' When Fogg tried to cover his ears, Luke snatched his hands away.

'Three . . .' The voice barked rhythmically, the cracks came as steady as a metronome. 'Four . . . five . . .'

'There are punishments worse than flogging,' cried Fogg.

'Are there? Then you could own up. They'd stop at once.'

The scourger paused briefly to shake blood and fragments of flesh from the whip; then raised it again.

'I know.' Fogg scarcely dared open his mouth for fear he should vomit. 'I know I should.'

The crack, the wrenching of the bowels, the echo, the remorseless counting, on and on. Fogg began to sag against the veranda rail.

'Only we're in a new world,' said Luke. 'It's an open page, and no rules.'

He turned away at last from the monotony of the flogging, from Charlton's bloody, torn back and the inhuman sobbing that slavered away into delirium; and contemplated the uncharted distances.

Moll said: 'You'll do well, *Mister* Firbeck. It's a bastard of a place. It takes a bastard to lick it.'

Jassy watched as her father took the sextant gratefully from Luke and turned it over in search of scratches or other damage. She hobbled towards her brother. He smiled a bleak smile, and for an instant she was not sure she knew him. Somehow he had aged many years overnight. He said:

'I'm sorry that was all I could recover. Your books, Jassy . . . they're all scattered by now.'

'There'll be others. Later.'

'There will.' Luke turned to his father. 'Will you take a reading?'

Jason trudged off uphill with the sextant, positioning himself on the ridge from which they had first viewed the land they supposed to be theirs. When he returned he was shaking his head in bewilderment.

'The configurations of the land conform precisely to those described in the grant.'

Samuel unfolded the parchment deed and held it open so that Jason could study it. Jason brooded over it, then turned reluctantly to Luke.

'There are signs of clearance,' he agreed. 'Of occupation.'

Luke began to laugh an ugly, uncontrollable laugh. Jassy longed to shut the sound of it out. It was too hateful, she did not understand it and did not want to.

'I see no cause for amusement,' said Jason stiffly.

'Oh, father, do you not?' Luke slapped him patronizingly on the shoulder. 'You bring us ten thousand miles, squander money on exhausted sheep, hire thieves to serve us, befriend a rogue because you fancy he's a gentleman . . . and harness our lives to a scrap of paper which proves to be worthless.'

'You accuse me? You dare to question my – '

'Our land,' said Luke, 'appears to be not our land at all. It has been taken. So what do we do now: what shall we do with the men already there?'

CHAPTER THREE

Colonel Pickering stared at his guest, then at his old friend, trying to make sense of either of them.

'*My* land?'

'It's legal, Harry, no doubt about it,' said Judge Glynne regretfully. 'I've seen Brisbane's signature a dozen times.'

There was a pounding in Pickering's head. Too much to drink this morning, that was the trouble. Often was the trouble. And a bit too much exertion with little Ellen last night. He was getting past it.

No, damn it, he wasn't He pushed himself to his feet and strode to the window in search of reassurance. He had cleared all that land, he had built this house, he was here and in his prime. The twenty or thirty people out there, dressed in their best, were all glad to know him and glad to be invited to his mansion and glad to drink his champagne. Who had created this oasis in the wilderness: who had made it what it was today?

'I do apologize,' said Jason Firbeck diffidently.

Apologize? Good God, no man got anywhere in this country by apologizing. Or by waving scraps of paper. You walked in and took what was there and got down to it and made of it what you wanted.

Look at that lawn: who had disciplined it like that in spite of the dry months and the floods and the rotten soil? And who'd had the money and the good taste to have those statues shipped all this way and set their whiteness against the fine red brick and spacious windows of the mansion? A mansion, a terrace, a lawn; an estate. He was colonel and squire and employer and a damn fine party-giver, if he did say it himself, and he was not going to accept defeat from a signature scrawled half a world away.

'Let me see.' He snatched the deed from Glynne and held it flat. 'And who suggested you should come and set up here?'

'Admiral Popple,' said Firbeck. 'I had the honour to serve under him. It was he who recommended me to Lord Brisbane.'

'Ever worked land before?'

'A small-holding in Yorkshire, sir. Fifteen acres.'

Fifteen! And here there were five thousand, every tuft won by bent backs and the sweat of honest men. Convict labour, yes – but he had treated his men well and they respected him. Between them they had won pasture from the bush in the days before there was any talk of land grants or documents and permits and all this rubbish. He remembered levelling the trees, and how you felled the end one of a row to bring the rest down like a pack of cards. Of finding a well, damming a stream, making pens and paddocks and huts and houses. Getting drunk with the men afterwards: they appreciated him all the better for that, and worked all the better. Fifteen years he had put into this place, and some of his convicts and ticket-of-leave men thought of it as home just as strongly as he did.

Glynne was watching him with a hint of pity in his face. Pickering wouldn't stand for that, not from any man.

He growled at Firbeck: 'You think you can manage in this climate, out here, in these conditions?'

Grapple with the drought of these last two years when the sheep died of hunger and rot, when you had to boil down carcasses for tallow. Face up to Government intrusions and the arrogance of the military, and the sudden outbreaks of escaped convicts going half crazy in the bush – outlaws ranging the scrub, not scared to rob and murder because nothing worse could happen to them. Was it like that on a Yorkshire small-holding? Silently he challenged the usurper.

'I have two fine sons to help me,' said Firbeck.

That was true enough. Pickering had shaken hands cordially with them before knowing the news they brought. The younger lad, especially, had a determined set to his head: had stared his host down as if to assert himself the moment he set foot in the house. An impertinent rascal, but a strong one. The kind of son Pickering would dearly have loved to have.

The long windows on to the terrace were open. One of his men walked past with a tray of newly filled glasses. The thought of just one of those glasses, of the prick of champagne bubbles against his tongue, was all at once more important than anything they had been talking about.

'I'm neglecting my other guests. Won't do, won't do. Let's go and join them outside. And later' – he drew a deep breath – 'we shall reach some agreement. If that's how it must be.'

God only knew how many parties he had given like this since the house was built. It was unthinkable that it should be the last. He nodded abstractedly to Judge Glynne's wife and to their pasty-faced, unappetizing daughter. The girl did not even notice. Her eyes were following the slow tread of the younger Firbeck lad. Dusty and unkempt in the middle of such elegance, he still had a disturbing masterfulness – the authority, thought Pickering dismally, of a man pacing out the measurements of his home, appraising this corner and that distant field.

'Well, Pickering, what's the prize to be?'

Young D'Arcy, strutting like a peacock in his dress uniform, had come to a halt before him.

'The race,' muttered the colonel.

'Indeed, sir. The race. Promised us something worth

running for this time. Can't keep it up your sleeve much longer, hm?'

The young man had been drinking heavily but his complexion was still fresh and his eyes clear. Pickering envied him. Envied every infernal one of them, younger than he and with so much ahead of them.

He snapped his fingers. 'Bring it out.' One of the servants set a tray down on the stone balustrade and hurried indoors. 'Made here by my own men,' said Pickering. 'Six months' work – and you'd go a long way to find craftsmanship like it.'

A group of convict workers moved deferentially closer at his signal, exchanging shy grins. D'Arcy scowled at them, then turned his attention to the table which was being carried from the house. On it stood a tall, fluted cup in embossed silver.

There was a gasp from the little crowd. Somebody began to applaud. Pickering beamed, and treated his convicts to a brusque little bow.

'The Pickering Cup,' he announced. 'All you've got to do is beat my horse. Beat Black Boongarre, that's all!' He laughed. 'You know the route. Round *The Trooper's Rest*, back here. Twelve mile, as near as dammit.'

D'Arcy said coolly: 'A tin pot.'

'What the devil d'you mean? It's pure silver.'

'Felon's trumpery. Wouldn't have it in me house.'

'Damn you, D'Arcy, you're insulting my men.'

'And damn you, sir, for insulting us with a trinket. Afraid of your horse losing, are you? Getting past it.'

'I challenge you, sir – '

'Harry!' Judge Glynne put out a warning hand, but Pickering brushed it aside.

He was aware of the travel-stained Luke Firbeck standing close by, his shrewd gaze appraising first one man and then the other, weighing the situation up.

'Put up something worth while.' D'Arcy raised his voice so that the hushed guests might not miss a word. 'If you're confident of winning your own race, don't see it matters what prize you risk.'

'Don't let him provoke you,' said the judge.

'Leave me be. All right, you name it, D'Arcy. I'll show you who's afraid.'

Yet he was beginning to be afraid. There was something sly and calculating in the twist of the young officer's lips – something he hadn't reckoned with.

'Something worth while,' D'Arcy mused. 'A race for . . . let me see . . .' Abruptly he pointed. '*Her!*'

Pickering swung round. His girl Ellen had been looking so proud, a minute ago, of her father's contribution to the fashioning of the silver cup. Now the colour drained from her pert little face.

'No,' she breathed.

'A convict girl,' said one of D'Arcy's cronies appreciatively. 'I say, what sport.'

Ellen's father stepped forward. 'No, master. She's our daughter, she's all we . . . you wouldn't let 'em, master.'

The convicts huddled together.

'Come on, now, D'Arcy.' Pickering tried to keep it bluff and man-to-man. 'Think of something else.'

'Afraid of losing her?'

There was a shock of silence through the gathering on the lawn. Did they all know, then: had they all guessed, and been laughing at him and his warm little mistress?

'Damn your eyes, D'Arcy.'

'A fair challenge. Are you going to accept?'

'Yes.'

One of the convict women let out the howl of a wounded beast. Two servants, convicts once themselves but with all the disdain now of liberated ticket-of-leave men, made a threatening movement towards the group.

'Don't send me away, master. Please.' Ellen was pawing at him, about to sink to her knees. 'We've been happy. I satisfied you, didn't I? Still do – isn't that right?'

Pickering wiped his left eye, which was beginning to water. Couldn't serve two mistresses, he thought bemusedly. He reached for a glass. The wine was cool and wonderful. At his age it was the women or the drink. Couldn't manage both.

But he could manage D'Arcy, damn his eyes. Had to. 'I'll beat the blackguard,' he said loudly. 'Black Boongarre'll show him a clean pair of heels.'

'Is it an open contest?'

The voice was that of Luke Firbeck. He was studying Ellen with an expression Pickering found almost as distasteful as D'Arcy's. Hoping to take her over with the house and estate?

He managed a nod.

There was noise and confusion and laughter again. Horses were brought round from the stables; one drunken guest practised ear-splitting calls on a post horn; the ladies gossiped, pretended to look shocked, pouted roguishly at the men.

Pickering poured himself a stiff grog before going out to mount his cherished, unbeatable Black Boongarre.

Unbeatable. Had to be.

Judge Glynne stood at the end of the line of horses. He raised his handkerchief; let it drop. D'Arcy uttered a mad whoop and urged his stallion forward.

They raced across the home pasture, over the rougher scrub and up the long eastern slope of the ridge. The direction of the village was marked by a smudge of smoke against blue sky. Then the downward path ran into tangled woodland and emerged above a stream. Sheep scattered as the hoofs of D'Arcy's stallion and the mighty Black Boongarre lurched down upon them. D'Arcy had taken the lead and was staying there. Pickering was unsteady in the saddle: the horse didn't like it.

A derisive shout trailed back through the trees.

Pickering moaned. Always been the best rider in the region, always had the best mount. And the best women. Now he saw himself running second, and a poor second at that. Sharing his bed with a convict's daughter – and even she was to be taken from him.

Two other riders were closing up from behind.

'Come on,' he mumbled, and swore. 'Come *on* . . .'

They scrabbled down the side of a steep gully and up the other side. One young fellow came almost alongside, tried too sharp an assult on the slope, and was thrown. Pickering was too angry – with competitors, with intruders, with himself – and maybe too drunk to laugh.

There had been times when he had pounded all the way to the village and back without ever seeing another horseman in front of him. In those days he had not met a rival until he was on the return journey.

This time it was D'Arcy who was already headed for home, delighted with himself, as Pickering galloped into the village.

He had to stop. Couldn't go on, couldn't complete the course without a breather.

A couple of children cowered back close to their shack.

Helmich came out on the top step of his store. 'So – there is another? What you think you are doing? Like madmen, storming in and out. You kill someone. You . . .'

There was an answering screech from the other side of the street. Pickering slid from his horse and smirked blearily at the woman on the veranda of the inn. Moll, good old blowzy old Moll, yelling over his head.

'Keep your tongue to yourself. They're the ones we make a living out of you, you and me. Trouble with you, you bloody foreigner . . .'

In spite of his gloom he could not stifle a chuckle. They were real, these two: flesh and bone of the world he knew, a world they had helped to make before a host of ineffectual newcomers tried to shoulder a way in. Moll and her husband belonged here, together and apart. Not living together for years now, but incapable of living entirely apart. Always within shouting range. Their abusive yells across the street were a daily and sometimes twice or thrice daily feature of life in the village.

'I will fetch soldiers,' Helmich was raging. 'There must be law and order, no? Look – another he comes!'

Luke Firbeck galloped down the street. He must have pushed his nag hard to bring it in like this. But it was badly winded, not up to the task.

The storekeeper waved to an officer and two soldiers who appeared from the far end of the street. They ignored him. As the officer jabbed a thumb at the frontage of the inn, one of his men held a post in place while the other hammered it into the ground and nailed a notice to it.

Moll, about to shriek some further insult at her husband, was drawn by curiosity off the veranda to inspect the board.

From where he stood, Pickering could read the words: Out of Bounds.

'What is out of bounds?' asked Luke Firbeck, reining in but not dismounting.

The officer, a podgy little man with a thick neck and surly eyes, said: 'Everything beyond this notice. The Government's defining new limits to the Nineteen Counties. About time too.' His Welsh accent rose in sing-song gratification. 'Settlers are no longer permitted beyond the official boundary.'

Moll spat in the dust. 'But look here, officer – '

'Captain. Captain Hopkins.'

'You're not trying to tell me, are you, that my inn – '

'On the wrong side. Out of bounds.'

The storekeeper burst out laughing. 'Oh, that is most funny.' He hugged himself. 'Most comical.'

'What about liquor?' Moll's ringlets shook in a fury. 'Men want their drink, you know. Your own men, for a start. They're not going to like this, I can tell you.'

'They can buy it from the store.'

'I'll give you bloody store . . .'

Helmich went on laughing uncontrollably. Moll paced towards him with a vixenish baring of her teeth. 'They'll not make an outlaw out of *me*, anyway. I'll just have to move back. In with you.'

'What?'

'Into your store. Back into your bed. Put up with your cold feet again . . .'

Helmich was no longer laughing. He went ashen. 'Captain, this is not possible. This I cannot bear.'

The paler he got, the more purple Hopkins became. He slapped his thigh and made a brief gesture at his men. Grinning, they tugged the post out of the ground and carried it behind the inn.

'My little joke,' gloated Hopkins.

'Joke? You think that's funny?' Moll let out a shivering sigh. Then, seeing Pickering at her elbow, she simpered. 'Ale, sir? Need one myself. Join me in some good ale?'

Behind a younger face flickered in the shadows of the doorway. There was the flash of a bare arm. It would be cool in there. Cool ale to wash grit from the throat, and then a warm body to rekindle old embers.

Pickering said: 'By heaven, you could convince me.'

Luke Firbeck seemed to have been mesmerized by the sight of the board establishing a new limit – or maybe by the rolling, untamed land beyond that limit. Now he shook himself and turned his horse's head back down the street.

Pickering said: 'You'll do no good on that old hack. Take mine.'

'I don't – '

'Take Boongarre, you blithering idiot. Tell 'em I fell. Thrown off. Very nasty. It's the *horse* that has to win. Nothing in the bet about who has to ride it. You can still catch that swine D'Arcy.'

Young Firbeck barely hesitated. In an instant he had swung across to Black Boongarre and was off down the street in a swirl of dust. It was a long chance, but the boy might still win. Not a horse in the Nineteen Counties, or outside them, to touch that one.

The girl was waiting in the doorway.

'All right, woman.' Pickering went up with Moll on to the veranda. 'If I'm going to take a tumble, lead me to it.'

On the homeward journey Pickering's bones ached and he felt as dispirited as the unresponsive horse between his thighs. Wouldn't be much use to Ellen tonight. If she was there . . . if he hadn't lost her by now.

Bumping down the last half mile, he saw the groups still drinking champagne on his lawn. And still laughing, louder and more hysterically than ever. They laughed even harder as he reached them.

'Master.' Ellen threw herself towards him.

He looked at Luke Firbeck, who shook his head. His expression was frozen. He didn't take kindly to defeat.

Gently Pickering disentangled himself from the warm, yearning girl. D'Arcy was ready to leave; and D'Arcy was smiling.

'You won, then?'

'I did.'

'You're taking her?'

'A bet's a bet.'

Ellen's hands twisted and pleaded.

'Can't renegue,' said Pickering.

The party began to break up. It had been a long day.

He called for more champagne, but by now there was a listlessness in the air. People had long rides, long drives, ahead of them. He urged some to stay overnight. But the chatter ebbed away, the carriages departed, the horses trotted off down the long miles to homesteads and the far township.

'*You* will stay under my roof?' said Pickering to Jason Firbeck.

'We have much to discuss.'

'Yes. Yes, we must turn our minds to it.' It was their roof rather than his that he was offering them. 'In the morning,' he said, stalling. 'In the morning.'

Before there could be any argument he set up a bustle of activity, choosing rooms for them, sending one of the younger girls to attend on Miss Firbeck, and promising dinner and more drinks before it was bedtime.

Only Luke Firbeck rejected the quarters he was offered. 'I'll sleep in the open.'

'Wouldn't dream of it. Plenty of room here.'

'I like to keep an eye on the sheep.'

'There's your shepherd. And I'll instruct my man Morgan to lend a hand.'

'I don't see myself,' said Luke remotely, 'ever lying at ease under this roof.'

Pickering stumped off to find Morgan. It struck him, through the vagueness of his headache and depression, that there were fewer of his men around than usual. Were the convicts brooding in their shacks, hating him for having gambled Ellen away?

He found Morgan and sent him off to give a hand with the Firbeck flock. Luke remained adamant: he, too, would spend the night close to the sheep.

Pickering wondered what dreams were stirring in that defiant head.

His own dreams were tumultuous. Three times he awoke

from a sickening confusion of memories and fantasies, and reached out for Ellen – to find that there was nobody there. Long before dawn he was wide awake, making plans for the estate because that at least kept the vision of Ellen at bay.

In the morning he took Jason Firbeck aside.

'I have a proposal to put to you. You're new here. It would be a fearsome task for you to take over the estate with no experienced man beside you.'

'I put my trust in the Lord,' said Jason.

'Yes. Quite so. A lot to be said for that. But you still need somebody down here with two feet on the ground.'

'This proposition of which you speak . . . ?'

Pickering hoped the man was going to be persuadable. Fellow had a perfect right, he supposed, to reject any compromise whatsoever and simply throw him out. But there was no harm in trying to salvage something from the mess.

He rang, and ordered a bottle to be brought in. He would feel more at ease with a glass in his hand.

As the ex-convict set a tray on the table and drew the cork, Pickering could restrain himself no longer..

'I offer you a partnership,' he said in as lordly a manner as he could summon.

The servant jangled bottle and glasses together. The tray gave off a long, singing note.

'A partnership,' said Pickering, 'in which you and I will work together, contributing our own special knowledge. You follow me? Put the place in good order for you after I'm gone, and for your family after we're both gone. But we don't want that to be for a long while yet, eh?'

He took the glass which was handed to him and looked over its rim at his guest . . . or partner . . . or dispossessor.

Jason Firbeck's bushy eyebrows seemed to clamp down more heavily above his eyes. With one hand he held his glass, but was not drinking from it. With the other he rubbed the silvered hair of his sideburns.

The servant backed away towards the door. Firbeck cleared his throat and said: 'A most considerate offer.'

The door closed.

'So we may start our discussion from there? Splendid.' Pickering drained his glass and shakily got to his feet to refill it. 'Of course there'll be details to work out. Have to have Glynne over here to prepare papers, tidy up problems, make sure nobody *else* comes along and . . .'

His voice trailed away. Through the window he saw a strangely funereal procession trudging down the last slope before the track turned in towards the house. He had been right about his convicts: they had been absent last night. Whatever they had been up to, their return was a slow, solemn affair.

With Ellen. Ellen was there.

And with a body laid out prone on a rough litter of branches and bark.

'What the devil . . . ?'

He strode out to meet them, with Firbeck at his heels.

The figure on the bier was that of Ellen's father. He had been shot at an angle through the shoulder: half his neck was blasted away. Ellen stood mutely beside the corpse as cortège halted.

'What happened?'

Ellen said dully: 'They came to bring me home.'

'You mean they set on – '

'At the ford.'

In a steady but lifeless tone she recited a story which by now seemed to have lost all meaning for her. Her father and his friends had set out before she had even left with D'Arcy. They laid an ambush at the ford six miles out. When D'Arcy and his two companions, joking and making foul promises to Ellen as she rode wretchedly between them, reached the river in the twilight they found large boughs blocking the way. D'Arcy and another man dismounted to struggle with the obstruction. The convicts pounced. Ellen cried to them to leave her be – she saw nothing but trouble for them. But her father and three others brought D'Arcy down and held him down and shouted at her to turn the horse and ride for home. She hesitated. D'Arcy broke free. He was armed: he shot her father down and kicked his way back to his horse. Two other convicts were injured – one in the arm, one in the hip – and then D'Arcy and his companions had ridden off. Without Ellen.

The dead man was brought home down the weary miles on a bier fashioned from the surrounding woodlands.

They buried him that noonday a little way from the house. As they looked down on the raw earth, Ellen raised her voice in a keening wail and intoned his epitaph:

'He *made* land.'

Luke Firbeck, who had been standing by the graveside with lowered head, looked up sharply and studied her with new interest – an awe.

Ellen was back. Pickering did not yet know whether D'Arcy would send to reclaim her. Perhaps the whole affair had gone sour on the young braggart. Or perhaps he would bide his time and find a way of seizing something else. Pickering had already lost so much to him in rash bets – a merino flock, a Brahmin bull, a hundred guineas. But he had not lost Ellen. Not this time.

In the evening, with the funeral behind them and no further excuse for delay, he realized that he must bring the whole Firbeck family into his confidence.

They sat in his drawing-room – so soon to be theirs as much as his – and Jason Firbeck announced the news.

'I can contain it no longer. Colonel Pickering has offered me a Partnership in his estates.'

Jassy Firbeck looked wonderingly, lingeringly, around the gracious room.

'*His* estates?' said Samuel softly. But Pickering had already deduced that Samuel was not the one whose opinions counted. He waited for Luke Firbeck.

Luke said: '*I* offer you . . . us . . . land we share with no one. Ours. With river, grasses, woodland where we need it and clearances where we don't. And *our* mark blazed round the borders. What do you say to that?'

'I say you must be demented,' said his father sternly.

'You sound grateful to Colonel Pickering. For what? We are supposed to thank him?' Luke leaned towards Pickering as if about to strike. 'Would you thank *me*?'

Pickering's stomach turned over. God, how he wished this bristling, snarling young pup could have been his son.

'Where's this land you speak of?' But he knew the answer already; remembered Luke Firbeck's rapt gaze, out into the unknown beyond the village. 'Set your sights on a place already?'

'Beyond their precious new limit.'

Pickering's desire to cling to his home was all at once meaningless. What he would most have loved would be to go off with someone like young Firbeck and start all over again, hewing a world out of a wilderness. There would be times when he might regret it. Days when this young lad would certainly regret it. Days when he would want the comfort of a home such as this. But – echoes from the past sang a wistful tune in Pickering's head – there would be more, far more, times when he would trample the grasses and hear the caterwauling of those damfool birds, and he would be able to hold his head high and declare *This is my land.*

'Squatters?' said Jason, outraged. 'You propose that we abandon civilization, defy the law . . .'

Luke turned to his sister. 'You'll come with me.' It was not a question but a statement.

'That she'll not,' said Jason.

'The grass is richer than here. And we shall build you a home you can clean, and where you can grow strong and be happy.'

'Enough of this. We already have a home, ready for us here. It is ours. We belong here.'

Luke had not taken his eyes off Jassy. 'Well?'

'Leave the child alone,' said their father. 'Here is where her future happiness lies.'

Luke waited.

Jassy said: 'I . . . I must go with Luke.'

'Then we'd best be making preparations.' Luke wasted no time. 'Go to the wagons. Tell Shep we'll be moving on in the morning.'

Jason said: 'You will give instructions to nobody without my authority.'

Luke towered above Pickering. 'I'll ask one favour, and one only, from you.'

'Likely as not I'll grant it.'

'Your man Morgan. We need another one such along with Shep. I'll take Morgan off your hands for a reasonable price.'

Jason tried to protest. Pickering shook his head and held out a stiff tot of grog. Jason tried to wave it aside. He would have to get used to it, thought Pickering. It was the only solace for an older man without strength in his mind or limbs any longer.

'Should you wish to follow – ' Luke's voice softened as he addressed himself directly to his father – 'I've no doubt they'll tell you at the village where we've gone.'

'This is intolerable. We came here as a family, and as a family we must stay together, we must . . .'

Pickering left them to their family conflicts, making his goodnights and escaping to his room.

Ellen was waiting for him. Ellen grave, her eyes still

swollen with weeping. But Ellen here, still with him, needing him now as much as he needed her.

He undressed, scratched his paunch, and wriggled into his nightshirt.

In the looking-glass he saw her watching him. Saw the shape of her, and wanted to weep, and knew he wasn't so old, not so impossibly old.

She said: 'That man's paper, his piece of English paper – '

'You've heard, then.'

'We have all heard. Word has passed among us.'

'Well, there we are. Must play the game.'

'Game? It must be always a game – always these strange rules?' The hair was falling over her smooth, naked shoulders. He could smell the muskiness of her. 'A game in which my father loses – and dies? And you know why he is dead?'

'Because he didn't understand that – '

'Because he understood better than you do. He believed in this place, and in you. And the others believe in it too. They came to rescue me because they knew it was wrong that you should give me away. And they do not believe you have the right to give *this* away.'

'They're forgetting themselves. They're still Government men, out on hire, here only for – '

'They think of themselves as *your* men. And I am yours.' Her voice became husky, insinuating. 'Haven't I made you strong? Helped you? Because I . . . I love you. We all do. We are your strength, and we will not give it to another.'

She unfastened the top lace of her bodice. He looked down, grateful for the steady pulse of his desire.

Between her breasts was a fold of parchment. She moved enticingly so that it crackled; and she laughed.

'So careless, that Mr Firbeck. He takes so much for

granted. And there is nothing here that must be taken for granted. Nothing that must be taken at all.'

In the morning Jason Firbeck walked from the house to the milling flock of sheep. Samuel was at his side, and Pickering and Ellen walked a few steps behind.

Luke shaded his eyes against the morning sun.

'Father.'

'You will see that I have changed my mind. You did not force my hand. I reached the decision independently of your precipitate action.'

Luke looked at Pickering with dawning wariness. The colonel held his breath. Jason Firbeck might be too proud to admit that he had lost his title deed; but if the son guessed, he was quite capable of abandoning all other plans simply in order to settle this battle and claim his father's rights.

'The act of a generous man,' Pickering ventured. 'A proud one. My heart goes with you.'

Jason looked at him, as suspicious as his son but with not enough conviction to frame a challenge.

'Ready to move, then?' said Luke.

Ellen's hand rested lightly within Pickering's elbow as the men, the girl, the wagons and the animals creaked and cracked and bleated out on to the trail.

Pickering gulped. 'He's not admitting he's lost the – '

'I think he has many blunders behind him. Another one such as this, and he'd lose the respect of his family.'

'You have no shame.'

'No.'

Without her at his side, he might even at the last minute have galloped after them and admitted the theft, implored them to stay, offered Luke Firbeck anything he asked.

Ellen nuzzled his shoulder.

Many times, he knew, she had hoped he would give her a

child. Unspokenly she had tempted him to sow his seed, to marry her and make everything secure for a future in which their son would inherit and there would be Pickerings on this land throughout the generations.

He wished it had been so. But it wouldn't be, not now. He was bitterly certain of that.

Luke Firbeck ought to have stayed.

CHAPTER FOUR

'He *made* land.' The convict's epitaph haunted Luke. His family saw that he was set on having it said of him in his own lifetime, not after a wretched death. If his only tools were their bare hands he would still make them tear a livelihood from the wasteland.

Samuel loyally deferred to their father in decisions on any question. But there was really no final decision until Luke had had his say. The men knew this, too: Shepherd and Morgan soon learned who to defer to and who to keep clear of if things went wrong.

It was Luke who drove them on. Luke who decided on the run of land which would best suit their purpose. Jason Firbeck protested several times along the way; but never fervently enough to bring the plodding caravan to a halt. They passed other squatters on smallholdings: some surly, with emaciated families and emaciated land to work on; some just dour, unattached men making shift with a few pigs and goats. A number had erected reasonably sound weather-boarded shacks. Most struggled on in turf huts or crude wooden shelters with uneven planks for a floor, strips of bark for a roof, bark curtains over window-holes. There was not a plough in sight. Men and their womenfolk chipped and scratched away with hoes; and the weeds and scrub pressed in on their pitiful crops.

Luke sneered and rode on.

Mosquitoes whined and stabbed from all sides. The only sure way of keeping them at bay was to smoke them off with burning sheep dung. At first the smell was intolerable. But after days and nights of being bitten mercilessly, you learned to tolerate anything that would conquer the swellings and blotches all over your body.

'Why must we go so far?' Jason protested. 'We shall need regular supplies from the village. If we're to have any kind of neighbourly life – '

'We can exist without neighbours,' said Luke.

'But what kind of life will that be? They say there are bushrangers in these parts, preying on anyone who wanders too far from official protection. Convicts on the run. The farther we go – '

'The farther we go, the fewer greedy eyes there'll be fixed on what we do.'

Luke's mistrust drove him as inexorably as his lust to make land. He wanted a good run, but a good one in the middle of bad land: an estate whose edges ran off into territory nobody else would want to touch. And not so close to the trading village and its barracks that eventually the settlement spread out to meet them. Government had declared a boundary. When it suited its greed, Government could equally well push the boundary farther out to engulf the squatters.

When at last they reached the spread which satisfied all Luke's demands, Jason was too weary to argue. If he found fault, they might be urged even farther away from the frontiers of more or less civilized settlement.

There were trees to be burnt and hacked away; scrub to be cleared; water to be found and channelled; and their own self-proclaimed boundaries to be established by blazing trees and putting up fencing. There were temporary huts to be erected, a house to be gradually assembled as the trees came down. For a time their tables were the boxes and trunks they had brought with them, their bedding the fleece of sheep and opossum skins stitched together.

Luke went to and from the village. He bought up the effects of a man who had gone bankrupt: a few battered chairs, mattocks, axes and shovels, a crate of chickens – precious little to show for a life's work. One day he returned with a magnificent bull, Caesar, roped through a nose-ring to the back of the smaller wagon. The gullies to the north of their range were crawling with wild cattle. They could be rounded up, a herd started: it would cost nothing but the grass they fed on.

It was always Luke who went on what Jassy called his shopping expeditions. Their father, he implied, would miscalculate, spending money as foolishly as he had been known to spend it before, or simply not buying the obvious necessities. Once or twice Luke took Jassy along and left her to spend a few hours with Anna, daughter of the German storekeeper; but rarely let her stray far from his sight and never let her travel alone. If his father craved companionship, that was his father's misfortune. Jassy needed it and Jassy should have it. Jassy was the reason for so much that Luke did.

Samuel wondered, sometimes, what would happen when Luke found himself a wife. Or Jassy a husband.

Samuel was contented enough with his steady, protracted task of blazing the boundaries. Stripped to the waist, he hacked through shoulder-high scrub and worked his methodical way along the bank of the sluggish stream they had chosen as their western border, chopping and burning the capital 'F' into one trunk after another. For nights at a time he did not return to the turf and bark shack he had made for himself beside the wagons, but slept under a blanket and ate and drank from a battered can. Together he and his horse paced out the miles, chipping a way round the long circumference of land they had claimed.

The stream made a convulsive turn between an upthrust of orange-red rocks. The vegetation was thicker, the monotonous oily green of eucalyptus broken by spurts of yellow flame tree and some scarlet-tongued shrub he could not put a name to. The rock was saw-toothed, with a few wide gaps. He kept his line of blazes as close to the natural barrier as possible.

Framed in one gap, right ahead, he found himself confronted by a shape which was not another rock formation and not a cluster of bushes. A small but sturdy shack was set against a slope, half hidden by gum trees and with a rectangle of cleared ground in front of it.

There was a flicker of movement. Samuel backed away to grope for his gun and adjust its sling over his shoulder, then went cautiously forward again. He stopped in the opening, leaning his right hand against the warm surface of the stone.

Below him, near a creek which must branch away from the meandering stream, a young woman in a shabby blue dress bent over a patch of newly turned soil, patting it down with a shovel. The shape was unmistakable, even if he had not so recently seen the burial at Pickering's. But this grave was pathetically small. At its head was a roughly fashioned wooden cross, adorned with a crumpled artificial flower which must have come from the girl's straw bonnet, lying on the ground near by.

Samuel's foot slipped. A cascade of small stones clattered down the slope to the creek.

The young woman stumbled to her feet and saw Samuel framed in the opening. He held out his hand to reassure her, but the gun slid forward and he had to crook it in his arm to steady it. The woman raised the shovel.

Samuel slithered down the loose stones. Her nerve failed her. She dropped the shovel and ran towards the hut, flinging herself in through the doorless entrance. When he reached it he found her crouched on the floor within, trying to load a rifle.

'Lay it down. You don't have to be afraid.'

The quietness of his tone got through to her. She cradled the gun across her body, but looked up and waited for him to speak again.

He said: 'I'm Samuel Firbeck. You're on Firbeck land.' He looked round the dingy interior, with a box serving as a table and a trimmed log for a seat. 'Is there anything I can do?'

She got up. Even in her dishevelled state there was no missing the supple contours of her body and the fine, defiant lines of her face.

'Oh yes, mister. Yes, there's plenty you can be doing. Bring my baby back to life. Give me my virginity back. Let me live my life the way it ought to have been. Can you do all that?'

He put out his hand to touch her. She misinterpreted the gesture and struck it away.

'Scum! Gentry . . . rotten gentry. Keep our men in chains, make manure of us to feed the lands – *your* land, isn't that what you said?' She waved out of the door towards the tiny grave. 'Oh, the crops'll grow fine, mister, with our flesh and bone.'

Gently he asked: 'Who's looking after you?'

She pushed the unkempt hair back from her face. 'I came to this cursed place' – it was like a recitation which she had not given for a long time but could put together again if she took it slowly – 'because I was sent here. By those who were looking after me, as you put it. Sent with other girls from an orphanage in Coventry. Told us we'd have a better chance out here.'

'Not a convict, then,' he encouraged her.

'No, mister, not a convict. Just an orphan they didn't want to pay for any more. I was fifteen. And on board ship they raped us. Me and the others, all of us. The sailors – week after week of them. And then left us to the mercy of the stinking streets. Sydney Town. Know what that means?'

He ventured: 'Your baby . . . ?'

'About a year ago I met this man. A real man. Told him I'd run away from my job – servant in a rich house, that's what I told him I'd been. And Tom believed me.'

'This Tom: a sheep man, or a farmer?'

Her lip curled.

'Ticket-of-leave man? A convict?'

'Tom loves me. He's gone to get supplies.'

'When did he leave?'

'A week. More. I don't know. We squatted here so I could wait for my baby. Didn't want to stay in the town, see: somebody might recognize me, tell Tom.'

Samuel had a sudden vision of Luke when he heard of this trespasser. There would be no compunction. She'd be driven off, and if her man was an ex-convict so much the worse.

So Luke must not know.

He put out his hand slowly so that this time she would have no fear. They shook hands with absurd formality. For all the grime bitten into them, and nails broken by the earth, she had beautiful fingers.

'I hope things go better for you, Miss . . . Mrs . . .'

'Nora,' she said. 'That's all.'

'Nora,' he said. 'When your Tom gets back, it would be safer if you moved on.'

She smiled wryly. As he turned his horse towards a gap in the bushes, she called after him: 'Not that way, mister. There's bog that way.'

'Bog?'

'Our milk goat sank in it. You should know about it,' she jibed, 'if it's your land.'

'Thanks.'

When he rode off he carried with him a lingering picture of Nora's wan but tempting face and the instinctive grace of her movements. If Luke asked what progress was being made along this boundary and wanted to check for himself, he would somehow have to be steered away.

Jassy wept. Her father planted himself before Luke, and raged: 'I won't have it. I forbid you to lay a hand on him.'

'He knows damn well who took Caesar, and I'm going to beat it out of him.'

'We saw enough brutality on our way through. I'll not have it brought into our own home.'

Morgan lay slumped against a stack of hurdles, his head bandaged with a scrap of blood-soaked rag. Luke pushed his father aside and grabbed the man's arm, dragging him to his feet.

'Tell me, or I'll cut you to ribbons.'

'I've told you all I know, mister.' Morgan was a big, hulking specimen, but there was no fight in him. 'I watched that bull o' yours best I could, never took my eyes off it. That's the truth. But I was knocked out, and that was that.'

'You let Caesar go. As good as gave him away.'

'I've told you, I didn't have a chance.'

'Honour among thieves, is it?' Luke rushed Morgan towards a tree. With one hand he tore the shirt from the man's back. When Morgan belatedly tried to struggle free, Luke smacked his head hard into the tree, then lashed his hands around the trunk. 'Don't betray your kind, is that it?' He stepped back and reached for his whip.

Jassy cried out. 'Luke, please. He's had enough.'

'This is the language they speak out here,' said Luke icily. 'The only language he understands.'

The whip whistled, and cut into Morgan's flesh. Morgan screamed.

Luke said: 'Who stole the bull?'

'How could I see? I didn't have a chance, I . . .'

The lash tore a fine ribbon of skin from Morgan's back.

'No, mister! No more!'

'Who was it?'

'I don't know. I swear it.'

'You know everyone hereabouts. I've heard you making a fine big song about what you know and who you know. So tell me who crept up on you. You must know his tricks.'

'No, mister.'

Another bloody gash was etched into his back.

'Shipton!' screamed Morgan. 'Tom Shipton, that's who it must have been.'

'A convict? Outlaw?'

'Went bush long ago. He can get through the country like a snake: never see him, never hear a sound.'

'Where will I find him?'

'If he doesn't want you to get near, then you won't find him nowhere.' Morgan faltered, hearing the butt of Luke's whip scrape meaningly on the ground. I've got an idea he's on your land, mister. By the shallow crossing.'

'You lying scum.'

'On the Holy Book.'

Luke tensed, lashed out one more stroke for good measure, then jerked his head at Shepherd. 'Cut him loose. And get the horses.'

Shepherd and Morgan, wincing, set out sullenly, falling far behind as Luke rode like a madman towards the distant ridges. When his horse stumbled he cut at its flank as savagely as he had cut at Morgan's back. They raced on.

Only when he was drawing close to the stream and its shallow ford did he slow, dismount, and tether the panting animal to a tree. Warily he went forward on foot, his carbine in the crook of his arm. A faint but steady wind stirred the bushes, keeping up a harsh rustle which muffled his footsteps.

On the wind he heard a woman's voice. 'Tom, leave the rest.'

'D'you know what they're worth? That new one alone's worth five o' the rest.'

Luke edged forward. Through a cleft in the rock he saw a half-concealed shack. Beyond it, hides were hanging out on a line to dry. The man and woman were taking them down and making bundles of them. As he watched, the man turned to face him. And saw him.

Luke flung himself forward.

The woman shrieked. Her man knocked her aside. She put out a hand to save herself, but dragged down the line of hides.

Beyond was another line. It carried the splendid, unmistakable skin of the bull Caesar.

Luke let out a roar like any bull's. He dropped his gun. He was going to finish this man off with his own bare hands.

Shipton met his mad onrush with a short jab that sent both of them reeling. Luke steadied himself and swung at the convict's stubbly chin. The shock of the blow ran up his arm. Shipton grabbed him and tried to beat him down to the earth. Luke kicked savagely, straightened up, began to punch Shipton backwards. They blundered over a soft patch of earth, and wood splintered under his heel.

'You bastards! My baby . . .'

Luke wavered; looked to one side. What baby? He saw a broken cross a few feet away. Off guard, he swung back too late. Shipton was swinging a heavy baulk of timber at him like a scythe. Luke ducked, but a great hammer struck him, red agony blazed, and then he was falling into darkness.

Pain dragged him back to consciousness. Faces swam before his eyes, spattered with aching explosions of light. He struggled to sit up. When at last faces came into focus he saw Morgan a couple of yards away, studying him with sly satisfaction. Beyond, Shepherd was forcing the struggling young woman away from the hut.

'Shipton?' croaked Luke.

'Always was a slippery customer. He'll take some finding out in the bush.'

'How long . . . ?'

'Found you lyin' here, we did. Couldn't have been long, because *she*' – Morgan jerked a thumb at the distraught woman – 'hadn't got herself ready to go. *If* she was goin'.'

Luke looked round for the horses. Morgan and Shepherd must have found his mount on the way and brought it with them: the three were tethered near by.

His eyes met the enraged eyes of the woman.

He said: 'Bring her along.'

'You'll get nothin' out of me, mister.'

'We'll see.'

Samuel stayed close to the homestead the next few weeks. Somebody had to, he told himself and his father. Somebody had to get on with building the house and supervising the stock, with Luke away all the time. Luke riding out with his obsession, staying away for days on his hunt for Shipton. Luke hard-mouthed and remorseless, insanely ready to take on an entire continent in his quest for vengeance.

Rumours came in from the village that Luke spent some of his fury on the girls in Moll's shanty brothel. If he had been asked, he might have replied that he was seeking news of Tom Shipton from the likeliest sources. But nobody asked Luke questions like that. Samuel was not sure whether Jassy heard the tales or not. If she heard them, perhaps she was able not to listen. When Luke did come back it was always Jassy he spoke to first. For a few seconds when they met he could dismiss the fury from his face. Briefly he became the gentler Luke they had known back in Yorkshire: a boy again, shyly adoring his little sister and shielding her from hurt and promising her the world – and the moon. Then the fever would burn up in him again. Settling the account for that stolen, slaughtered bull was what mattered most. Others could look after the sheep, dig up the earth, work on the home he had promised Jassy. Nothing could distract him for long until he had tracked Shipton down.

In the hope that the man might be lured back to rescue his woman, Luke had Nora virtually staked out like a decoy. Day after day she sat in the open peeling potatoes, scrubbing clothes and clumsily sewing for Jassy, with someone always on guard.

But Shipton did not come. From her cynical eyes it was impossible to tell whether she expected him or whether she knew he had left her for good.

Samuel contrived to work near her whenever there was a plausible reason. That way, Morgan or Shepherd could be released for other duties. It fitted in well enough with Luke's orders. And it fitted in with Samuel's own desires.

He liked to believe that Nora was less tense, less filled with hate and despair, when he was close to her. When he spoke, she answered at first in monosyllables. Then, by the third week, she was reluctantly answering, though giving nothing away. And her eyes were answering his, evasively yet with a dawn of something she didn't want to trust.

In Luke's absence, Jason took Jassy into the village for a night, to talk with Anna while he bought seed and paint, fresh fruit and more nails for the house. They returned escorted by Lieutenant Robarts, who showed a partiality for Jassy's company which she gave no sign of reciprocating.

Luke rode in from the bush a few minutes after the family had sat down to eat. Nora ate alone and apart, sitting by the stone base of the half-finished fireplace.

Luke acknowledged Robarts with no more than a sketchy pretence of courtesy.

Robarts said: 'Still looking for Tom Shipton?'

Luke grunted.

'What would you do if you caught him?'

'Kill him,' said Luke.

'And face a murder charge?'

'For defending what's mine?'

'The magistrates don't like squatters,' said the lieutenant bleakly. 'Legally you don't exist, and the land isn't yours. A murder charge is just the sort of excuse they need to remove you. Fortunately,' he added, 'someone else has saved you from your folly.'

Luke froze. 'What are you talking about?'

'Shipton's dead.'

There was a long howl from Nora. She let the plate slip through her fingers to the floor, and rested her pale brow against the raw new stonework.

Luke said: 'It's a trick.'

'His musket,' said Robarts, 'his clothes, his corpse – found in the Parramatta river and identified by two convicts who knew him well.'

'God rest him.' Jason bowed his head.

Luke said: 'May he roast in hell.'

Nora was trying to control her sobs. Samuel slid away from the table and put his hand on her shoulder. She flinched, and mutely shook her head.

'Death's not enough!' Luke bellowed. 'I'd like to get my hands on his stinking corpse, skin it the way he . . . he . . .'

Jassy stretched out her arms imploringly.

'This place,' said Jason, his head sinking over the table as if to say a belated grace: 'it turns us against all that is good. We're not what we were.'

That night Samuel took Nora into his bark hut. And the next night, and the night after that. Jassy slept in the one bedroom so far completed under the temporary roof of the house. Their father slept under the same roof, on an improvised couch by the fireplace. Luke lay sometimes under a lean-to near the sheep pens; sometimes in places far away about which nobody asked. Samuel had his hut. And now he had Nora.

She rarely spoke. Her powers of speech were numbed. But, pounded by the stabbing heat of him, she occasionally let out an uncontrollable moan, and when that happened his own ecstasy flooded through him like scalding lead: when he drove into her he was driving out the past, he would make her forget, she would hunger for him and only for him. Tom Shipton was dead; but her appetites weren't dead.

Luke was now too often at home. With no one to pursue, he had to turn his relentless energy on his own folk. Samuel was driven back to the boundaries, to chip blazes on a thousand more trees. Morgan and Shepherd were harried from dawn to dusk. Even Jason was not exempt. Luke offered suggestions about useful occupations, little jobs that needed doing, with a son's deference and a grown man's contempt.

And he knew about Samuel and Nora. He withdrew his orders about guarding her every hour of the day; and intimated by a droop of his dark left eyebrow that, although she was always wrapped in a blanket under the dray by sunrise, he knew full well where she spent her nights.

One morning, newly returned from a trip to the village, he stood with legs wide and arms folded as Samuel crawled out of his bark shelter.

'D'you know what the woman of yours is? A whore. A paid bloody whore.'

'Keep your voice down.'

'A brothel wench. I saw some sketches of her – oh, mighty pretty little drawings, by God they were.'

'Which shows only where *you* spend your time.'

'One of Moll's bitches for a month or two. On leave from the city, you might say. You didn't know that, did you?'

'Yes,' said Samuel, 'I knew.'

It was good to catch Luke off balance for once.

Samuel went on: 'She told me all about it, quite some time ago.'

'And still you tumble her in there – or under the dray, or . . . wherever the heat comes on you?'

'What's past is done with. What chance did a girl her age have, shipped out at the mercy of riff-raff who . . . like . . .' He could not finish. 'I'd like to give her a chance of something different now,' he managed at last.

'That's nothing to what she'll give *you*.'

'I love her, Luke.'

Luke's rages were dangerously close to the surface these days. A deep crease bit into his forehead. 'Love? Love such a . . . You think I'll have her here? Here with Jass? On my land?'

'It's not your land. I'll talk to father.'

'Talk to God if you like. And see what response you get. I tell you she's not staying.'

The two brothers confronted each other. Then Samuel wrenched himself away. In any fight between them, Luke would inevitably have won. But that was not what stopped him: it was the sheer sickness of it, the thought of the two of them fighting; when there were so many other enemies in this hostile land they needed to fight, shoulder to shoulder.

He walked towards the dray under which Nora would be sleeping if Luke's abuse had not awakened her. Two hours ago she had crept from his hut with a drowsy little murmur and a lingering touch of her hand. Already he longed to see her sleepy, sated face again. He stooped, half propped against the wheel, and gently tapped the huddle of blanket.

It gave way. Aghast, he snatched it back.

Where Nora should be was a sack of chaff, plumped to resemble a sleeping body. A few bits of clothing which Jassy had given to Nora were folded into the shape of a pillow. And there was a torn sheet of paper with a scrawl of unsteady handwriting on it.

'Something wrong?' It was Luke, lounging beside the dray, with unforgiving relish in his voice.

Samuel read the scribbled words and read them again and made no sense of them. *You are a kind man but no good to me in any way. Goodbye mister.*

'Gone?' said Luke. He slapped Samuel's shoulder. 'Best thing she's ever done, or ever likely to do.'

After they had eaten, Luke snapped finger and thumb at Morgan and ordered his horse to be saddled. It was not until he was turning the chestnut's head towards the far watercourse that he announced his destination.

'Going to burn down the shack. Shipton's thing.'

His father shook his head. 'There's a sight more important things to do than that. No need for it.'

'That shack,' said Luke venemously, 'is an open invitation to anyone who rides this way. We're not having squatters on our run, nor anywhere near it.' He urged his horse on to the dusty track they had worn towards the north-west. 'If you see smoke, don't worry!'

He went off at a leisurely pace, implacable, in no hurry now that he had ordained how the last relic of Tom Shipton should be wiped out.

Jassy was feeding the chickens when Luke returned. She was startled by the flurry of his arrival, so different from the easy-going canter of his departure. Her father came round the house to see what the commotion was.

Luke said: 'She's back. That woman, Nora. Back there as bold as brass, in the damn shack.'

'The poor creature maybe wants to settle everything up. Nowhere else she can be with her memories.'

'Memories!' snorted Luke. 'I'll tell you something. Shipton's still alive. She's waiting for him.'

'But his body's been identified.'

'Look, d'you think I can't tell between a woman in grief and a woman waiting? She's *waiting*. So I'll have a bite to eat and then I'll be off to Parramatta.'

Jassy turned away, sickened by this rekindled greed for vengeance. There were times when she felt that, like Nora, she must run off and be on her own and wait . . . but wait for what? Some impossible daydream that would never materialize?

She heard Luke say, in a more restrained tone: 'Father, keep Samuel away from the shack. Send him off to mark the southern boundary. No need for him to know she's still around.'

'You're determined to go, then.'

'I am.'

After gulping down a plate of damper and cold mutton, Luke was off with renewed speed and vigour. Not one to give up, thought Jassy fondly and fearfully. Land or his fellow men, he had to beat them both. The salvation of the Firbecks – if he didn't destroy himself first.

CHAPTER FIVE

Parramatta, some fifteen miles inland from Sydney, was a steadily expanding township with some aspirations to set itself up as the effective capital of the colony. Stage coaches ran twice daily between the two places, suitably armed against the highwaymen and footpads who harassed the main road; the spacious hotel which formed the Parramatta terminus was as fine a piece of architecture as any such in Sydney. There was a large barracks and smart administrative offices. Along every street the brick and white stone buildings of prospering merchants and contractors were going up, overshadowing the earlier wooden edifices.

The approaches were less fine. Luke Firbeck rode in past a string of rum shanties, from several of which cheerful, obscene insults were shouted at a road gang of convicts, obviously old acquaintances of the drunkards – and likely to be acquaintances again, by the look of the drunkards and the look cast on them by a mounted trooper.

There was also the Female Factory, across the river from the town, replacing the makeshift prison and workhouse for women which for too long had shared premises with the men's prison. The new building and new conditions had done little to improve the language or disposition of the occupants. Raucous screams from barred windows followed Luke towards the bridge. A dozen women filing out of the main door whistled hopefully after him.

'Make an offer, sir? Make a bed for me?'

'Keep you warm, sir.'

There was a cackle of laughter, broken by a more

plaintive voice: 'I was a good girl back home, sir. Marry me and I'll show you how good I can be . . .'

It was drowned in a gust of derision.

Luke had heard that this was a good place to come to find a wife. Or simply a companion, to share the rough times and slave beside you. You got loyal service. A woman who had once lived in the Female Factory would do anything for a man rather than be sent back inside.

He was not desperate enough to contemplate such an alliance.

Reaching the market place, he had to rein in to avoid a shambling procession of male convicts, chained together, gaping about them with a curiosity turning to despair. They were obviously new arrivals; and obviously could tell at a glance that there would be little alleviation of their cruel lot in this place.

'Mr Firbeck!'

Drawn in to the side of the square, as if to avoid contamination from the wretched creatures trailing past, was a trim open carriage. Luke gazed blankly at the shadowed faces of two women under their frilled parasols. Then the younger one's giggle, as fat and squirming as the girl herself, reminded him of Colonel Pickering's lawn. It seemed such a long time ago now.

He lifted his dusty hat to the mother. 'Mistress Glynne, isn't it?'

'And Caroline,' said the judge's wife archly.

The girl leaned forward with a hopeful smirk.

Her mother said: 'You'll be in town a little while?'

'I have business to see to. I'm not sure how long it will take.'

'But we must see you while you're here. Dine with us. You must, truly you must. Shall we say about six?'

It was difficult to frame an excuse on the spur of the

moment. And one never knew: Judge Glynne might prove useful in his quest.

'Thank you, ma'am. Your servant, Miss Caroline.'

The carriage moved on, the two ladies smiling and putting their heads close together under their parasols.

Luke inquired the way to the court house, and presented himself with scant ceremony to the records clerk, who wore a serge jacket and loose blue trousers which were clearly meant to suggest a uniform. He bristled with authority.

'I assure you, sir' – it was off his lips as soon as Luke had finished speaking – 'there can be no mistake.' He flipped open a ledger and tapped it triumphantly. 'Thomas Shipton. I wrote it down myself.'

Luke restrained his impatience. 'But there'd have had to be some proof.'

'Indeed there was. The gun, with his mark on it. Clothes which had often been seen on him – and he didn't have that much of a wardrobe! Two of his cronies – we've no reason to distrust them – both saw the body and identified it as Shipton. What more do you want?'

'To identify him myself.'

'The coffin is closed.' The clerk's manner became unctuous. 'Sinners we may be in life, sir, but in death a man's fate is out of our hands. I cannot allow Shipton's coffin to be tampered with. Most unseemly. He'll be buried this evening, along with a convict lass and her offspring. May they rest in peace.'

He closed the book. Luke fumed, half reached out to grab the man and shake agreement out of him bodily; then knew it would be only asking for trouble.

He stamped out.

Not every petty official in the town could be as sanctimonious as that little hypocrite. Somebody, somewhere, could be tempted: if not by reason, then by the chink of money.

Luke found the morgue, a timber and plaster building in a squalid back lane. It was ramshackle but capacious: along with the men's and women's prisons it did some of the briskest trade in the community.

He tugged the bell rope of a side door, and heard the jangle within. Footsteps shuffled close, then went away. He pulled again, and rattled the door.

At last an ageing face, coarse with grey stubble, peered suspiciously out.

'What d'you want?'

'Let me in.'

'Mercy be, I can't do that.'

Luke took out a gold coin and turned it so that a slanting ray of the afternoon sun struck sparks from it.

'You'll get me into trouble,' said the old man feebly.

'Are you going to let me in?'

The door creaked open. The man looked away from Luke as though pretending that if he didn't see him, there could somehow be nothing wrong about the transaction. But his right hand was firmly thrust out. Luke dropped the money into it and walked on.

A sickly sweet smell fouled the room beyond. A number of wooden slabs were laid across low trestles, three of them occupied by roughly hewn coffins. It was so gloomy that Luke called for a lamp. The man scurried after him, snatching a lantern and tinder-box from a shelf.

'Which one is Tom Shipton?'

The old man was beginning to regret the whole thing. 'It'll be me in one of those meself if I get copped.'

'Which one?' growled Luke.

The man gestured to the nearest coffin.

'Open it.'

The smell intensified, sweetness turning to corruption as the lid squawked open. Luke clapped a handkerchief to his nose and leaned over the corpse.

When he stood back he said: 'That's not Shipton.'

'Who else would it be? I don't make no mistakes.'

'Somebody did. Somebody made a very big mistake.'

Luke was striding towards the door. The morgue attendant bobbed after him, whimpering his greed. Luke tossed him another coin and went out into the fresh air.

The tricky bastard. The clever, tricky bastard. Where was he?

He thought of the hut, and Nora waiting. He was eager to jump on his horse and ride back over the mountains, down through the canyons and on across country until he reached the hovel and wiped it out, wiped out everything and everybody connected with it.

But he had promised to dine with the Glynnes. Now he wished more than ever that he had been able to dodge the invitation. Judge Glynne was no use to him now. And his fat, simpering daughter was no use and never would be.

It would be bad policy not to appear, though. These fussy lawyers and officials had a stranglehold on England and were already trying to fasten one on New South Wales. If there had to be a collision, the Firbecks would take up their positions. But it was foolish to invite ill will without any immediate good cause.

Grudgingly Luke presented himself at the Glynnes' trim brick house, with its gleaming white veranda and gleaming white tablecloth and white napkins, and the gleaming pinkness of Caroline.

There was another guest, a man of Judge Glynne's generation, with a cavalry officer's moustache and rheumy, querulous eyes. Introduced as Mrs Glynne's brother, he greeted Luke civilly enough but viewed him warily throughout the meal, and stiffened when their hostess began to build up a calculatedly flattering picture of the Firbeck fortunes.

'Your father must own a vast area by now, I fancy, Mr Firbeck?'

Luke desired only the end of this stuffy evening. Bluntly he said: 'We are squatters, ma'am.'

'Ah, yes, but *gentlemen* squatters. There's quite a distinction, is there not?' She beamed at her daughter, and at her husband, who nodded.

Her brother evidently saw no such distinction. 'Too many of 'em out there,' he snapped. 'Far too many. Setting up on their own, draining the colony.'

'We're suffering from a shortage of labour,' the judge hastened to explain to Luke. 'Geoffrey blames the squatters.'

'Walking off, sitting down where they choose. Should stay this side of the mountains, build the place up.'

'A fresh consignment of men came in today,' Mrs Glynne ventured. 'Caroline and I saw them.' Both ladies permitted themselves a genteel shudder.

'Picked up two myself,' said the judge. 'One of 'em's sound enough. Devon man, a blacksmith. Ran into more trouble than he bargained for – got mixed up with some of those union conspirators, didn't realize what he was doing. He'll settle in all right.'

'But watch that other one,' rumbled Geoffrey. 'They told me you'd made a bid for him.'

'The north country fellow?'

'That's the one. You know who he is, don't you?'

'Can't say I – '

'He's a Shipton. Another of 'em. Brother of that blackguard Tom Shipton. Could almost be his twin.'

Luke had raised his wine glass to his lips, half listening, trying to estimate how long it must be before he could decently take his leave. Now the stem cracked between his fingers. A trickle of blood ran into his palm.

Old Geoffrey was rambling on. 'Transported here for poaching. No respect for property. Just like his brother before him. A plague in their own county, and now we get 'em shipped out here for us to discipline.'

Luke brushed aside Mrs Glynne's flustered exclamations and stemmed the flow of blood with a napkin. He leaned across the table.

'You're certain – about Shipton?'

'My overseer knows how to handle that kind. Discovered they value the skin on their backs.'

'Uncle!' Caroline protested, with an apologetic pout at Luke.

'Tom Shipton's brother,' mused Luke, deliberately echoing the mistrust in Geoffrey's voice. 'A feller like that'll take some handling.'

Judge Glynne shifted uneasily in his chair.

'A hundred stripes,' rasped his brother-in-law. 'And that'd be only a beginning.'

Mrs Glynne looked apprehensively at her husband.

Luke said: 'Judge Glynne, may I ask you a favour?'

'By all means, my boy.'

'I'd like to take Shipton off your hands.'

'He's mad,' said Geoffrey. 'But take him up on it. Quickly. Before he changes his mind. Put the Blue Mountains between him and us.'

Glynne sought some sense from Luke. 'It's clearly important to you.'

'I've one or two scores to settle. In memory,' said Luke heavily, 'of his brother. Out where we are, it won't be too difficult to teach him a thing or two.'

Geoffrey regarded Luke with new respect.

'But,' said Luke, 'I could do with some . . . let's call it bait, shall we? If I put him through it and he comes up to expectations, could you arrange for him to be pardoned?'

'Oh, I say.' Geoffrey's opinion plummeted again.

Luke shamelessly treated Caroline to a winning smile. She went an even deeper puce than usual, and twittered at her father:

'Papa, with your influence you know you could.'

'Hm. Well, yes, I suppose . . . mm, I could draft some sort of conditional pardon. With suitable safeguards, of course. But' – he was still baffled by Luke – 'why should you want to run such risks with Shipton? If anything goes wrong, you're beyond our jurisdiction . . . beyond *any* jurisdiction. No law to help you. You wouldn't prefer me to find you someone who – '

'What's his full name?'

'Er . . .'

'Charles Shipton,' barked Geoffrey.

'Charles Shipton.' Luke savoured the name.

'I'll sign a transfer for tomorrow morning, then,' said Judge Glynne.

'So Mr Firbeck must stay the night,' his wife rushed in. 'You *will* stay with us, Mr Firbeck, won't you?'

'And if you need an escort, at least to the limits – '

'No escort,' said Luke quietly. 'I don't need any escort.'

The hut was still there. Nora was still there. She sat dabbling her feet in the stream. Every now and then she looked up at Morgan, in the shade of a gum tree with his gun across his knees. They made a strange tableau as Luke edged his horse over the loose shale of the ridge.

Morgan got up thankfully. Even a hated boss was better than the unchanging routine.

'There's your rations.' Luke flung a cloth swag down beside him. 'She tried anything?'

'Nothing, mister.'

'If she does – '

'Look, mister, I know about if she does. But what if she *doesn't*? If she don't try a bolter – just sits there – what 'appens to me?'

He had raised his voice. Nora got up from the bank and called bitterly: 'Then you rot away here till you die, cully. Isn't that right, mister?'

Luke turned his horse back the way they had come.

'I've been meaning to thank you, Luke Firbeck.'

It was an unexpected shot. Luke reined in and glanced back across the stream.

Nora laughed. 'Thank you,' she cried, 'for letting me know Tom's still alive.'

He rode off before he said something he might regret; something that would tell her too much. She was sharp, the bitch. Sharp to realize that this renewed watchfulness could mean only one thing. Well, let her sweat it out. He'd tell her no more. If anyone cracked under the strain, she had to be the one.

He wondered, as he had wondered a score of times this last week, whether Shipton had somehow writhed his way back through the bush to that shack, unseen and unheard.

Only one man was good enough to make sure that didn't happen. Luke made a long detour, well away from Nora and the shack, to reach him.

The sun was warm on the grass outside the cave. Inside it would be cool. Charles Shipton was one of the lucky ones: not breaking stones in the heat and horror of a chain gang, but lying at his ease in the shade, waiting to do the skilled job he was best qualified to do.

'You, there.' Luke slid from the saddle and climbed the last steep ledge of rock to the opening, carrying another swag of food. 'Shipton!'

Nothing moved. There was no one there. Not a sound. Until a hand touched his shoulder. Luke swung round, ready to swing the cloth swag like a weapon and follow up with a swift right punch.

Charles Shipton grinned at him. 'Told you I were best poacher in the Dales.'

Luke forced an answering grin. This was the man he had chosen; and he had chosen right.

Charles Shipton was uncannily like his brother. They

might, as Mrs Glynne's brother had said, almost have been twins. But Charles was subtler, more feline in his movements. When he opened the cloth and took out a chunk of cold meat, it was done with a silent twist of the fingers, a flick of the wrist like some travelling conjuror's dexterous feat.

'Mister.' He looked up with something more than respect – something that offered friendship, if Luke had been prepared to accept it. 'You're sticking to your word. And the other bit – about me getting a pardon if I do this job for you – that holds, too?'

Luke drew a parchment from his back pocket. It was a deed of pardon, folded in two. He tore it neatly along the fold and handed one half to Shipton.

'The other half you get when it's finished.'

Shipton picked a sliver of mutton from between his teeth. 'Aye. But this man I've got to listen for. What's he done to you?'

'He's a thief. And a killer. If he's not killed first, he'll kill. You or me or anybody. All I want is to know where he is and when he's going to show up.'

It was not the uncompromising deadliness of it that perturbed Shipton. He nodded amiably enough, but asked: 'What if he's not killed, though? I don't fancy being sent back. Not to be a convict. I'm looking to find my brother. Tom an' me, we get on. A sort of feeling we got. When I find him we'll start afresh, make a go of it.'

'You will?'

'Maybe if I was to satisfy you . . . I mean, once we've done this job of yours, you'd help me find my brother?'

Luke was silent.

'You'd like him,' said Charles Shipton.

He waited for some comment. All Luke could say was: 'Do the job and you go free. That's our bargain. Right?'

'Right.'

Luke gazed out over the treetops, over the scrub and the indigo haze. Somewhere out there . . . or, for all he knew, crouched somewhere behind him in the rocks . . .

He said: 'You swear there's still no sign of . . . of this one I'm after?'

'He's about,' said Charles Shipton calmly.

'Then why the blazes didn't you – '

'Last night. And the night before. Took some of my food. A real sly partridge of a man – and a hungry partridge.'

Breath whistled slowly out between Luke's teeth. 'That's not the only thing he's hungry for.' He waved down towards the two diminutive figures moving out of shelter for a moment, then disappearing near the stream: Morgan dogging Nora's footsteps but keeping his distance. 'Sooner or later he'll go down. She's got a body a man'd risk his life for.'

'But not you?'

'Not me,' said Luke frigidly.

'I reckon I've got the measure of him,' Charles Shipton hesitated. 'But just for the sake of it, who *is* he?'

'The less you know about it, the better for you in the end. Just get him when he comes, that's all I ask.'

'I'll get him. I know his ways. But tell you one thing – he don't have a gun.'

'How do you know?'

'If he hates you like you hate him, he'd have picked you off long before this.'

'There's a full moon tonight.'

'I'll get him,' said Charles Shipton again.

The silver brightness of the moon cast huge shadows under the rocks. Here and there a sluggish ripple glinted on the water and then was gone. The evening breeze had died away into the bush by nightfall. There was no sound save for the occasional rustle of some nocturnal animal scuttling to safety.

A shadow moved.

Tom Shipton waited for a cloud to cover the moon. It was a long wait. The clouds were high and wispy, and there was little wind up there to drive them.

He would get to the hut this very night. Twice he had set off into the west, telling himself Nora wasn't worth the risk – too much of a burden for a man who wanted to travel light – and twice he had turned back.

There was a long, rippling snore. So much for the guard placed there by Luke Firbeck.

And if Firbeck himself showed up, so much for him too. This time it was all going to be settled. Though why there should still be this vigil, why they should still be mounting guard when he was supposed to be dead, Tom Shipton couldn't fathom.

What designs did Luke Firbeck have on Nora?

The sheer physical ache of it drove Tom on.

Less than a quarter of a mile away another shadow detached itself from the rocky hillside and then was lost again in the bushes above the stream.

Charles Shipton knew his quarry was on the move; and knew the direction he was heading in.

They were drawing closer. And if the man was as clever as Charles knew him to be, he must also sense it by now. Something you couldn't explain, except to one of your own kind. And that fellow out there was one of Charles Shipton's own kind. But there weren't going to be any explanations between them. That wasn't the deal he had made – the deal he proposed to honour.

He slid the carbine from his shoulder and sidled forward. The outline of the shack was dimly visible.

Suddenly a dark figure shot up from the ground as fast

as a kangaroo rat, and made a run for the ground beyond the rocky spur.

It was not what Charles had expected. Instinctively he whipped up the gun and fired. Echoes bounced back deafeningly from the low cliff.

He thought he heard a woman cry out. Then it was choked back. So that was where Luke Firbeck was waiting – in the hut, silencing Nora . . . and waiting.

Ahead there was the crack of a dry branch. A pause, a faint scuffle of feet. And stillness again. He was uneasy. Right up through his nerves, through his skin and finger-tips, he felt that he was being lured on. His prey was taunting him, coaxing him into some place where the hunted might become the hunter.

A step at a time. Head on one side, testing every resonance of the night air. A long wait. He could stand motionless for hours if he had to.

Somewhere to his left a branch fell with a thud. Charles bent almost double, made a swift dash at it; then knew he had been tricked. The branch had been tossed from somewhere else. He might already have passed the man: could have been fooled into doing precisely that. He took a tentative step forward, but the ground became unexpectedly marshy. He stopped. The moon was threatening to come out full from behind a cloud. Before him were no bushes, no hints of shadow.

From his right came a faint plopping sound, seeming to mock him. Before the moon could emerge, he ran towards the noise.

His burst of speed lasted only a few seconds. The ground sucked at his feet and imprisoned them. He sank to his knees, letting go of the gun; and the wet, sticky grip caught his knees as well and began to devour them.

He spread his arms forward, trying to spread his weight. But when his outstretched palms touched the surface, the plopping of the mud told him where he was.

He had floundered into the heart of a swamp.

He tried to turn, to twist round. Tried to gain the strength to paddle with his arms and take some of the weight from his sinking legs.

The bog reached up for his armpits.

The moon came out.

A dark figure stood confidently on the edge of the dark, foully glistening patch. A knife gleamed in his hand.

'Sorry about this.'

The blade sped with deadly accuracy. Blood choked in Charles Shipton's throat.

'No. No . . .' He heard the bubbling hopelessness of his own voice. 'Oh, be with me, mother . . . Mother Shipton . . .'

'What was that?'

Now he knew the voice from the bank. And as the moon rode out full and inescapable, he knew the face. He must be mad. Dying in a last, nightmare delirium.

'Tom! Tom, you . . .'

'Charlie.' His brother put a wary foot on the mud and began to edge out into the bog, testing each step. 'Charlie, it's me, how did you . . . God, how could this . . .'

It was useless. Charles Shipton heard himself spluttering for help, to be lifted out of this slime, to be saved . . . please . . . Tom . . . *please* . . . Then his head dipped forward and the huddled corpse was little more than a dark mound in the heart of darkness, surrounded by an agitated bubbling.

Tom Shipton raised his head to the night skies and let out the roar of a wounded animal.

Feet pounded down the slope. In the moonlight Luke Firbeck lurched towards the swamp.

'Did you get him? Did you?'

But there was a fleeter figure, running desperately, with a gun. 'Tom – *Tom*!' Nora threw a rifle. It twisted in an arc over the swamp and fell with a splash, too far away from

Tom Shipton for him ever to reach it. He floundered out of the morass, his hands splayed, going for Luke Firbeck.

There was another man there. Morgan, dragged from sleep, swinging his rifle up to his shoulder.

Tom Shipton was clear of the mud. He saw Firbeck's face right before him. All that was left in the world now was to smash that face to pulp.

'You,' he roared. 'You – you set my brother, my own brother, you . . .'

Morgan fired.

Tom Shipton stopped and bent over on himself. Then he crumpled to the ground.

Luke stepped over him and looked out across the bog. There was not so much as a hummock left on its surface. From his pocket he took the folded half of Charles Shipton's pardon which he retained. Wrapping it round a large stone, he tossed it into the swamp and watched it sink.

Nora was crouched by Tom Shipton's body. 'Dead?' It was too much for her to grasp, this second time, this death all over again. 'Tom . . . Tom . . . ?'

At last she became aware of Luke standing above the two of them.

He said: 'Now. Get off *my land*.'

CHAPTER SIX

Luke pushed the borders of his kingdom out and yet farther out. Word got round that the Firbeck estate was a rough one to work on, and the young 'un a sight too free with the lash. Labour was difficult to come by, and only a hard core of men stayed any length of time. And hard was the word for most of them. When the leader of a gang of ticket-of-leave nomads tried to bluster in and take over the homestead, there was only one law to set against them: the law of swift retaliation, with no rules and no mercy, enforced by defenders who were, just as much as the attackers, outlaws. When there was a dam to be built, complicated manoeuvres and bribery were necessary to hire convict labour which officially ought not to have been employed in the wilds without the Nineteen Counties.

Jassy watched her father and brothers make the land and make a home. They bred sheep, fattened cattle, sold hides, made money. It was what they had come here to do, and they were well in their stride. Yet where was the end to it? There was no promise of anything, tomorrow or the day after, but drudgery and conflict. It was a harsh land, soaked in the misery of its earliest settlers. And a treacherous land. There was drought, when the stock wasted and died. There were outbreaks of scab, when entire flocks had to be destroyed, and the sickening stench of burning flesh hung over the countryside for an eternity. After each disaster they started again; but could so easily be smitten again. And always there were mosquitoes, and bouts of stomach trouble, and festering sores, and the jeering of alien birds and wild dogs all around.

Something splendid might be fashioned out of it one day: but would she see that day? Her father's slow, generous smile grew rarer as the months added up to years. Luke's eyes darkened too often now with smouldering fire. His lips twisted with inward hurt, and the urge to inflict pain. He would not be thwarted or argued with. When he and Samuel were away, the place was empty. Yet it was easier to be without him: easier to be rid of his hectoring presence, his rudeness to their father, and the explosions of his wayward rage. Any tenderness still in him was reserved for her; but there were more and more times now when she could no longer be the shy, adoring little girl with him – times when his brutality repelled her, and disturbing times when she read a new, hurtful, unbrotherly need in his eyes.

Doggedly Jassy scrubbed, knitted, darned, cooked, tended the chickens and the vegetable patch, and cut up meat. This was what she most detested. She had lost count of the number of carcasses she had hung by their hind legs from the cross-bar and butchered. Still she could never become used to the fat and the blood and the smell of it.

One morning she stopped between one job and another, wiping one hand up and down her slimed hide apron in a kind of trance. Suddenly she felt, in spite of the great arch of the sky and the rolling countryside reaching for the far horizon, that she was in a trap. There was no way out, nor ever would be. She plunged her arms into the bucket and watched the water turn dark crimson. When she had washed the blood away she walked up to the house. Here they had worked wonders. It looked so solid, so very nearly respectable. The timbers, struts and planks were firm and proud; the roof was no makeshift thing but a stout protection against storm, blown sand, and rain. The heavy stone chimney at one end was by way of being a local landmark. From the flagged stone veranda one had a wide-ranging view of Firbeck land, changing under every whim of sun, moon and cloud. It was the palace Luke had promised her. She was growing to hate it.

Her father was not indoors. She changed into her green print dress, drew her hair tightly behind her ears and set her bonnet carefully above it, and hurried out before anyone should ask where she was going. For she did not know where she was going: knew only that she must walk in the shade by the stream, where she would not see a sheep carcass or the house or the expanse of scrub from which Luke would ride out when it suited him. Their way of life was what Luke decreed. There would be no easement, no variation, no end until it suited Luke.

The slow music of the brook calmed the resentful flurry of her thoughts.

If there was no happiness here, where else could she hope to find it? The village was still only an outpost of civilization, and a pretty unsavoury one at that. Luke, she knew, occasionally went there whoring; but it offered him or Samuel no other occupation. And they would be even less at home in the growing townships. Although the men might go to markets and sales in Parramatta and even as far away as Sydney, Jassy had paid few such visits. Each time there were startling changes, difficult to grasp after long exile in the hard, unyielding world beyond the Blue Mountains.

Ex-convicts prospered in trade, built themselves more splendid homes than many of the administrators and free settlers; and wreaked their revenge for past humiliation by calculated slights and sharp practices. They were called 'emancipists' by those who found it advisable to stay in their good graces. The military were not happy with this gradual levelling-out; but an officer's pay gave him little chance to compete with the newly emerging people who saw themselves as the true founders of the colony, the ones who had established it by back-breaking work and now deserved its fruits. Last-ditch social battles were fought to maintain or establish new distinctions between families of the original free pioneers, the emancipists, and upstart newcomers. The new settlers learned to counter with sly insinuations about the probable ancestry of the self-appointed 'ancient nobility' of the colony.

Jassy saw little of this for herself, save when it provoked grotesque imitations in the village between its garrison, the convicts and the ticket-of-leave men, and the few large landowners of the region. Whenever they met, Anna loved to report some new absurdity, some fine flourish of pretentiousness. And Luke occasionally brought stories back from the town, telling them with mounting scorn.

'Already they want to make the same pattern here as we suffered at home! Officials puffed up with their own importance, mock gentry grubbing for the privileges they fancy are their birthright . . . They want our wool now – and want to drive us off our land when they've taken all they need. They crippled our old country and they'll cripple the new one. Take what *they* want, on *their* terms . . . as if God gave them some special right to rule the whole world, for ever and ever, world without end.'

'And don't you, in your own way, wish to do the same?' his father once asked, sadly. 'Aren't you preparing for a private war, just as wicked and self-seeking as the old ones you used to condemn?'

Their voices seemed to ring in Jassy's ears, above the gentler plash and tinkling of the water over stones. She walked with her head down, wanting to be cleansed of the animosity and unending struggle.

'Good morning.'

This was no lingering echo. It was a clear voice from no more than a few yards away. Jassy gasped, steadying herself as her foot slipped a few inches down the bank.

A young man in his middle twenties was standing with a

notebook in one hand, apparently interrupted in the middle of some calculation. His mouth seemed to droop sceptically, drawn down by a curve of golden-brown moustache. His face was shadowed by a luridly dyed leather hat with a rakish brim. At first sight, in shirt sleeves and with a rumpled red neckerchief, he could have been some bush desperado. Jassy took a step backwards, ready to turn and run.

'I'm sorry. I startled you.'

When he raised his hat the shadows fled from his face, and the downturned lips quirked into a courteous smile.

'You did,' said Jassy crossly.

'I must say, I'm a bit surprised myself, finding someone like you out here.'

'We live on the ridge.' She nodded through the trees.

'You must be squatters.' When she did not reply he said, with a shake of the outrageous hat: 'My name's Elliott. Lieutenant Edward Elliott of the Surveyor General's department.'

'Jassy Firbeck.'

'How do you do.'

'But what does the Surveyor General want out here? I understood we were . . . well, out of bounds.'

'We have to map the interior for His Majesty. God bless him. And one hears rumours that in due course there may be some relaxation of the present regulations. It's said that once the dimensions of the problem have been established, the Government may be prepared to rent land to squatters, under reasonable supervision.'

'After letting us do all the hard work, they fancy setting a tax on us?' She thought of Luke's reactions if such a proposition were put to him.

'Which would entitle you,' said Lieutenant Elliott, 'to military protection, representation on the legislature . . .' He shrugged. 'But that all lies in the future. Captain

Hopkins would deny that it ought ever to come about.'

'Captain Hopkins?'

'My commanding officer. He's working in from the far side of the hill. Probably be along shortly.'

His eyes were both shy and quizzical. He was reluctant to turn away and continue with his work. And Jassy was in no haste to retrace her steps now, back to the house and the unvarying routine.

She said: 'You must be living under canvas.'

'In company with a million mosquitoes.'

They both laughed ruefully. Abruptly she heard herself saying: 'You could dine with us.'

'Oh. Thank you, that's most . . . but really, I wouldn't want to . . .'

'It would make such a pleasant break for us.'

'It's very thoughtful of you. Very.'

Now she was eager to be away, to tell her father the news and clean the place and make sure it was worthy of such a visitor: somebody from outside, somebody with a warm smile and polished manners, and such a different way of looking at her.

That evening he appeared in uniform, tightly buttoned and with his head held high. He was more handsome than she had thought. The two guests made a fine blaze of red and black and gilt against the dark wooden background of this main room – the Firbecks' sitting-room, dining-room and, all too often, debating chamber.

Captain Hopkins was too fat for his uniform. He had a face like a scarlet frog, his fleshy neck squeezed in by a tight collar. Sweat trickled from his cheeks on to his epaulettes. He had a grudge against the world – against the higher command which had failed to recognize his qualities and promote him, against the folk in Sydney with all their airs and graces, and equally against the settlers and squatters he met on his travels. Lieutenant Elliott had been right: Captain Hopkins certainly did not favour any concessions to squatters outside the Nineteen Counties, or any notion of bringing them under the protection of His Majesty's forces. Blandly disregarding the situation of his host, he declared himself in favour of exterminating all squatters, runaway convicts and bushrangers – whom he classed as one and the same – and only regretted that no one would authorize him to set to work.

'I've seen men with only half my talent promoted twenty times. No gratitude. I was in the Peninsula. Wellington, you know. I've done my job under fire – and where's my reward?'

Elliott leaned forward to pick up his glass, contriving to make an apologetic grimace at Jassy. The candle lamps trickled little rivulets of shadow down the smiling creases of his face.

Jason said: 'You have your family with you in Sydney?'

'Like yourself, sir,' Hopkins grunted, 'I'm a widower.'

'I'm sorry.'

'Damned dysentery.' Hopkins turned his perspiring face towards Jassy. 'Have you had it, girl?' Before Jassy, embarrassed, could find an answer, he let out a contemptuous snort. 'Course you have. Dribbling. Damned country.'

Elliott scraped back his chair. 'My tobacco is of considerable strength, Mr Firbeck. I wonder if I might smoke a pipe of it on your veranda?'

Jason welcomed the interruption. 'By all means.'

'I'll come with you.' Jassy spoke on impulse, anxious only to escape Hopkins's disagreeable company. When her father looked startled, she said meekly: 'May I, father?'

He hesitated; but his glance from her to Hopkins and back showed that he understood. 'Just for a while.'

It was cooler outside, and very still. The aroma of Lieutenant Elliott's tobacco was a new element in the all too familiar surroundings. She was content to fall into step with the young man and pace slowly up beside the stock pens. A horse whinnied, and she stopped to stroke it.

'You've not said a word,' Elliott commented.

She had somehow not wished to make an effort. Now she must try. 'Have you . . . er . . . have you been long in New South Wales?'

'Three years.'

'Oh.'

There was a pause. Elliott went on, awkwardly: 'The survey has taken me to most parts of the colony. The scenery is not so varied as that of England.' Obtaining no response, he said: 'In fact the scenery is remarkably unvaried. The gum trees and the burnt grass.'

'Yes.'

'But no doubt you have discovered in them their own beauty?' He tamped his pipe, stooped to see her face as the two of them became used to the faint light from the night sky. 'You have not.' he decided.

'No. I hate it.'

Jassy turned back towards the house. He hastened to catch her up. 'Have I offended you?'

'No, of course not.'

But she was quickening her pace, because she had said too much and it would do her no good, would do nobody any good, and she could not understand why her heart was beating so. She hurried; stumbled, almost fell; and hobbled towards the steps of the house, her hip and leg dragging at an angle.

'Miss Firbeck.' Elliott had no difficulty now in overtaking her. 'I apologize. I didn't notice. You've hurt your foot.'

Tears stung her eyes. She jerked her head away, tripped again, and then reached the veranda. Light flooded out through the open door. She plunged into it as her father was rising from the table.

'Jassy, is something the matter?'

Blinking against the brightness she saw Captain Hopkins patting his gross belly and leering at her. 'Young whipper-snapper misbehaved himself, has he?'

Jason took a pace towards the door as Elliott came in.

'Mr Firbeck, I don't know what I said to your daughter, but – '

'Whatever it was, sir – '

'Did you touch her?' snarled Hopkins.

'Of course not.'

Jassy reached the far door and fumbled with the latch to let herself through and find solace in the darkness of her cramped, tiny room.

'Exposed yourself for what you are,' Hopkins was ranting. 'Good family, all your fine airs, flaunting your so-called knowledge at us . . . knew it all along.'

'Sir' – Elliott ignored his superior officer and addressed himself to Jason – 'I still cannot imagine what should have caused such distress. Your daughter and I discussed the Australian landscape. Perhaps I bored her. I am not a witty man. Then when I saw she was hurt – '

'Hurt?'

'She must have twisted her ankle. I'm afraid I did not notice at first.'

Jason Firbeck let out a long sigh. 'Lieutenant Elliott,' he said quietly, 'my daughter is a cripple. Has been so since birth.'

Jassy wrenched the door open and found her way, knowing every step in the darkness, to her room and her pallet and her misery.

The musket shot stilled the humming countryside into a brief silence. A stutter of echoes rolled down an invisible canyon; and again there was nothingness.

Luke and Samuel, bent over their cooking pot on the

smoking fire, stood up simultaneously. Luke snatched up his billy, removed the pot, and poured water over the flames.

Samuel, hungry and disgruntled, trod out the ashes. 'You've told them shoot to kill, I suppose?'

'One sheep,' said Luke, 'one black. It's a fair price.'

They mounted and rode off in the direction of the shot. The place did not take long to find. Two sheep lay prone beside a rocky bluff, each with a native spear protruding from it. In the lee of the bluff was a flimsy lean-to, a skeleton of branches and bark against a background of mellow green and mauve jungle. There was no sign of life near the shelter; then up through the bushes came Shep.

'Did you get 'em?' Luke shouted.

'Too quick for me.'

'But what about *him*?' Luke gestured at the lean-to. 'What's he supposed to be doing?'

'Didn't stop to talk. Saw them blacks down the slope there, and went after 'em.'

They turned towards the lean-to.

'He the one we engaged that last trip to Parramatta?'

'That's him, mister.'

'Forgotten his name.'

'Harry. Scotch Harry.'

'I'll harry him, letting them creep up on him like . . .'

Luke stopped. They had reached the edge of the dry straw thrown down to make a rough carpet and a bed. Sitting up, propped against one of the wooden uprights, was the shepherd. His eyes were covered in flies, and his flesh was beginning to blacken and putrefy.

'Oh, Jesus,' said Shep softly.

Luke stepped over the straw and prodded the man with his right boot. For a second the body remained in its seated posture, then keeled slowly over. Two spears were driven deep into its back.

'We'll have to take him with us,' said Samuel, gagging. 'Give him a decent burial.'

'In that condition?'

Luke kicked straw and scattered twigs into a hump around the corpse, and pulled down the brittle bark roof. He stooped close to the edge and lit it. Flame ran into the heart of the kindling, and in a matter of seconds was licking at clothes and flesh.

'Harry what?' asked Luke, straightening up.

Shep averted his eyes. 'Scotch Harry.'

'I mean his real name.'

'Don't know as he ever had one.'

The funeral pyre blazed as they rounded up the sheep. The flock could not be left here: would have to be driven closer to the homestead until a new man could be hired.

When they were on the move, Shep said reflectively: 'It'll be the women done for him, I reckon.'

'Women? Out here?'

'He liked his velvet, you ponder my meanin'. Black velvet specially.'

'If he was on those terms with them –'

'Probably trod on somebody's patch. They're not a specially savage lot – don't go in all that much for gettin' their own back, like – but I suppose they could get as jealous over their womenfolk as anyone else, now and then.'

'Not specially savage?' Luke echoed ironically. 'Those dead sheep were just an accident?'

'Maybe meant to drag them off but didn't get the time. They don't understand about the likes of us – like you, I mean, mister – *owning* things. I been here long enough to learn that. They've been used to wanderin' about, settin' up camp where it suits 'em and livin' off whatever came to hand – stayin' or goin', just as it suited 'em.'

'It doesn't suit me.'

'So far's they're concerned, animals belong to everyone. Like the land.'

'This land belongs to me,' said Luke. 'So did those sheep.'

'They don't understand.'

'They'd better learn.'

Progress over the ragged terrain was slow. In the early twilight Samuel pointed out the glow of a camp fire half a mile or so up a bank to their right.

'Reckon we'll steer clear of that.' Shep diverted the flock a few degrees to the east.

Luke, without consultation and without issuing any orders, rode off towards the brow of the low hill.

Men rose to their feet as he reached the fire. In the shadowy bushes, darker shadows of women cowered back. Eyes gleamed at him out of the sombre dusk.

An elderly man with a bone necklace planted himself in Luke's path. In spite of his defiant stance his voice was wheedling rather than combative.

'Whitefella bring bacca?'

'No,' said Luke, 'I do not.'

'Grog?'

'No.'

'Should bring grog.'

Luke said: 'I've brought you just one thing. A warning.' He waved back over the darkening ranges. 'Sheep. Understand sheep?'

The chief pursed thick, leathery lips.

'I think you do,' said Luke. 'Sheep.' He raised his gun. 'Keep away from my sheep, or thunderstick go bang. Bang-bang. Understand?'

The only answer was the sputter and crackle of the fire. Luke wrenched his horse around. It shied, and nearly knocked over a sly-eyed, crouching girl who had crept inquisitively nearer. She sprang away, her breasts tightening and gleaming in the firelight.

Luke calmed the horse and urged it into a gentle trot downhill. Once he looked back. The girl was standing against the skyline, watching him.

Black velvet. A change, he imagined, from the raddled pink pulpiness of Moll's shanty whores.

He slept badly under the stars that night. Long before dawn he took over the last spell of guard duty from Shep.

They set out towards the river in a morning haze, to find the approach to the ford blocked by two redcoats adjusting a theodolite. The sheep floundered to one side and another. Cursing, Shep pursued the runaways.

'Get out of the way!' Luke roared. 'Off the crossing!'

A corpulent officer emerged from a tent. 'Stay where you are. We have work to do – delicate computations.'

'Step aside, sir.' Samuel splashed into the shallows.

'I'll do no such thing.'

Luke rode down on him. 'Who the devil are you?'

'I am Captain Hopkins, an officer of the Crown. And I give way to no damned outlaw.'

Shep was turning the strays back. They came running along the bank and smacked full into the tent. It went down, taking a collapsible table with it. Luke and Samuel circled round the troopers to round up their animals, ignoring the enraged shouts which followed them.

'Blithering jackanapes . . . have you in irons . . . see you in gaol for this . . .'

The water creamed to foam as the sheep careered and bleated their way to the far bank.

Luke glanced back over his shoulder. 'And what do you suppose that Welsh oaf is doing so far from his home comforts? Let's hope *he* runs head on into the aborigines.'

Jassy stirred a wooden spoon into the stew, savouring its

appetizing smell. When she turned her attention from the fire and the saucepan it was to find Lieutenant Edward Elliott's gaze fixed earnestly upon her.

'This is the first time in my life I have sat in a kitchen.' He set his elbows on the scrubbed table. 'I find the experience very profound.'

'You're mocking us.'

'On the contrary, Miss Jassy. I'm regretting so much of my life that has passed – so much without meaning.'

Nonplussed, she busied herself setting out plates on the table, making a clatter with the spoon and pan, and with knives and forks from the kitchen dresser which Samuel had fashioned with such loving seriousness.

Elliott said: 'Miss Firbeck, I owe you an apology.'

'I am sure none is called for.'

'The evening we first met, I offended you. I didn't understand.' Jassy shook her head, but he went on: 'I am ill at ease, I know it. An uncomfortable man. I come from a tolerably well-to-do-family – perhaps they shielded me too much, and at the same time allowed me too few simple pleasures. Such as sitting in a kitchen with a beautiful girl who . . .' At last he checked himself.

'At home in England – you had a comfortable home?' Jassy glanced despondently about the square, stark kitchen. 'Grounds, I have no doubt – a large estate?'

'Kept much neater than your kingdom,' he conceded. 'But with less love in it.'

'Not my kingdom. Luke's.'

'Luke?'

'My brother. You have not yet met him.'

'No,' said Elliott thoughtfully. 'No, that is yet to come.'

These past three days had been days stolen from ordinary time. Their conversation was stilted and commonplace enough, and sometimes they hardly spoke at all. And then she would catch herself revealing things which she had told nobody else; and would fall silent, and turn away; and his gentle voice would take up the thread and twist it enchantingly into another pattern.

Soon Captain Hopkins would return and demand what his subordinate had been doing with his time.

And Luke and Samuel would return.

Today Elliott took his midday meal with them, then went off to complete, he said, a map section. She wondered how much work he really achieved: surely very little, since he was so soon back, and as the shadows lengthened was closeted with her father. The earnest murmur of their voices fretted at her as she sat on the veranda, trying to read in the fading light.

Jason came out at last and stood behind her chair.

'Jassy. He wants to marry you.'

The numbness in her fingers almost made her drop the book. She got up, fumbling for words. A ridiculous shiver ran through her body and she drew her green shawl about her shoulders.

'He has asked' – Jason drove it home – 'to marry you.'

'You . . . you didn't lead him to suppose I . . . you didn't say I . . .' Suddenly she was mortally afraid. 'You didn't send him away?'

'He is still here. Waiting for an answer.'

'But father, do you think . . . ?'

'I think his motives are entirely good. He is a wealthy young man, and a sensitive one.'

'Don't you want me to stay with you?'

'For your own sake, my dear . . .' He, too, was finding difficulty with his words. 'This life is not for you. I have known that long enough. You should go. And go quickly.' He took her arm. 'Shall we go in?'

'No.' As he looked at her in surprise, she said gravely: 'I'll go alone, father, if you please.'

He stood aside and she went into the house. In the living-room a lamp was set in the centre of the table. Edward Elliott had been pacing up and down. Now he came to a halt.

'Miss Firbeck. Your father – he has told you . . . ?'

Mutely she nodded.

'Miss Firbeck.' His hands implored her, the declaration poured from him. 'I cannot explain the attraction of two persons each to the other. It is a joy we must take on trust. If it seems to have come too quickly, that should not be taken as an error, or . . .' He stopped, and laughed. She realized how much she adored that rueful laugh of his, and the gentleness in his eyes. 'That's book talk, isn't it? Enough, then. I love you. Will you marry me?'

'You can't love me.'

'I find it easy enough. Almost too easy.'

'Our acquaintance is too short. As you yourself said – '

'As I said, I love you. And I think you love me.'

She fended this off, not ready to admit to him what she had not yet admitted to herself. 'How can I leave my family, my home . . . all this?'

'You hate it.' He set himself before her, inescapable and insistent. 'Please be sure of one thing: I do not offer marriage from any misguided sense of pity.'

'Pity?'

'Because you are a cripple. Is that what you have feared?'

'I . . .'

'You need not fear that with me. Between us it is nothing. You love me,' he challenged.

'Yes.' It was so much simpler to say it and bow to the frightening truth in it.

'Come away with me. From this place. Marry me.'

She nodded.

'Say it,' he commanded.

'Yes.'

'Yes what?'

'Yes,' said Jassy, 'I will marry you.'

CHAPTER SEVEN

Luke roared: 'And you let them go? You let them go?' He stormed into Jassy's room and stared incredulously at the empty shelves, the tidily made-up bed. 'How could you – what possessed you?'

'They waited two days to make their farewells.'

'That's not what I meant, and well you know it. You let him take her – our Jassy.'

'I weighed the matter carefully,' said Jason, 'and gave it my blessing. I believe she'll be happy and . . . protected.'

'Protected? What was wrong with *my* protection?'

Jason tried to remain calm in the heart of the whirlwind. 'Lieutenant Elliott has means, and a position. His wife will be secure, happy and sheltered. I let her go because it was my right as a father to do so. It was not an easy decision. But I made it with love.'

Luke had sent his hat spinning into a corner of the room. Now he retrieved it and clamped it on his head.

'Where are you going?'

'To find them.'

'What good will that do?'

'Hasty decisions, taken behind my back . . .'

Luke was gone.

Jason sank into a chair by the table. 'I acted for Jassy,' he said, pleading for an answering nod from Samuel. 'If they had waited any longer . . . if Luke had created a great scene when he got back . . . her courage might have failed her. She would have lost the happiness that is offered to her.'

Samuel said: 'Father, I think she may have gone because she hates the life we lead here.'

'To some extent, but – '

'What if she doesn't love him?'

The sun through the trees made a latticework of shadow. Jassy ran into the light and out of it again, laughing. Edward trampled after her, dodged round a bush, and caught her in his arms.

'Well, Mrs Elliott . . .'

'Well, Mr Elliott.'

'Shall we be married in Parramatta?'

'Yes.'

'Shall we have children?'

She blushed, and smiled, and rubbed her cheek against his. 'Yes.'

'We'll have a very proper establishment in the most proper quarter in town. And join the fashionable Sunday afternoon promenade.'

'I'll make jams for the old ladies.'

'I'll be polite to the bishop's wife.'

'Oh, it should be England,' cried Jassy. 'To have an autumn when the leaves fall . . .'

He looked searchingly into her face, so close to his. 'You're very beautiful.'

Then he tensed. Far away there was the sound of hoof-beats along the track through the woods. Jassy was about to speak, but he put two fingers on her lips. The pounding came nearer, and through branches and tendrils of bush they caught a glimpse of two horsemen. Captain Hopkins and Luke Firbeck.

Jassy gasped.

Edward murmured: 'That was your brother?'

She nodded unhappily.

'Riding with Hopkins. Not a combination which promises

us much goodwill.' The sound faded away. Jassy slipped from his arms and walked back to their horses. He said: 'You've no regrets?'

'None.'

But the magic had been shattered by those pursuing hoofbeats. The idyll could not last forever out of space and out of time. Reality had to be faced.

They rode for a long time in silence.

Edward broke it. 'I fancy we shall find your brother waiting in the village.'

'Waiting?'

'Asking questions. And waiting for you to say goodbye.'

'I've said goodbye.'

'Not to your brother.'

Her head sank. They went on another mile, and again it was Edward who had to break the silence.

'I think this is something you must face. With me at your side. I must report my movements to the barracks. You must say what has to be said to Luke.'

Of course she had known all along that it must come to this. Her father had wanted her to hurry away, as if flight would somehow solve all problems. She had taken his advice with cowardly relief. And these last few days she had pretended that she and Edward could go on living just for each other, that her old life had ceased to exist. If, even now, he had asserted himself and said they must avoid the village and ride on to Parramatta, she would have seized the chance of deferring to him and avoiding Luke.

Yet at the same time she longed to see Luke, to face him and explain to him and win his blessing.

Edward came to a halt at a fork in the track. He glanced at her. She could offer no preference; wanted the decision to be made for her.

They took the path towards the village.

Jassy felt herself sway in the saddle as they rode down the

street. She conquered the moment of dizziness and forced herself to sit proud and upright, as befitted the wife of a distinguished young officer of the Crown. For although there had not yet been a formal ceremony – how could there be, out in the bush? – she was assuredly his wife, and intended the world to see it.

Intended Luke to see it.

Luke was standing by the steps of the store, talking to Anna. Something Anna said must have drawn his attention to the new arrivals: he turned very slowly, and stared at Jassy. She waited for him to speak.

Instead, he spun on his heel and crossed the road to the inn. She thought she could see him in the gloom beyond the window, peering out but wishing not to be detected.

Anna was tugging at her ankle. 'Jassy, is it true? What I have been hearing, that you and . . .' She waved towards Edward Elliott.

'Yes, Anna, it's true.'

'Oh, Jassy, I'm so happy for you.'

Jassy dismounted, still looking at the inn.

There was a sudden flash of red in the doorway – red jacket and red, puffed-up face. Hopkins came blundering out, suffused with drink and bad temper.

'You!' He brandished a fist at his lieutenant. 'You are under arrest.'

'On what grounds?'

'You have deserted your post.'

'So, sir, have you. You are also drunk.' Edward leaned down, and Jassy stood up on tiptoe so that he could kiss her brow. 'I shall be in the barracks.'

She nodded. He watched her for a moment, deeply concerned, as she walked slowly towards the inn; then rode off towards the barracks, ignoring Hopkins's ranting and spluttering.

Jassy stopped on the veranda to take a deep breath, and walked on into the tap-room.

As her eyes adjusted to the sombre interior, she saw Luke in the middle of the room – large, dark, hostile. She shook her head in a slow, silent plea, and held her arms out. In an instant they flew together, and he was kissing her. She was so happy. Then frightened, trying to pull away. 'No, Luke.' His arms were not the reassuring arms she had known as a child. His kisses were urgent and demanding. She was bruised by the uncontrolled passion of them.

'I love you,' he said hoarsely.

'I know, I know. But Luke, dear Luke – '

'I cannot bear that someone else – '

'Please. *Please*. You know that . . . anything else . . . is impossible.'

'Nothing is impossible.'

'Yes, Luke, it is.' She freed herself from his brutal embrace. 'I love him.'

'No.'

'And he loves me.'

Every straining, outraged nerve in his body tried to deny it. His burning gaze ordered her to say she was lying. A vein throbbed in his left temple. Without warning, something cracked inside him and he brushed past her, out of the door and up the street towards the barracks.

Jassy ran after him. 'Luke . . . you must listen . . . you must understand . . .'

Fast as she might run, he was some distance ahead of her when he reached the door of Lieutenant Robarts's office. She heard a buzz of conflicting voices, and the door was still swinging open when she reached it.

'What the devil do you mean by bursting in like this?'

'Out of my way.'

'Luke' – Robarts came round his desk – 'you cannot expect me to – '

'This man has taken my sister. They plan to marry.'

Jassy said: 'Luke, please.' She advanced into the room. 'Edward – my brother.'

'How d'you do.'

Edward put his hand out. Luke took a mighty swing at him, but anger made him clumsy. Edward stepped to one side and briskly knocked him down. Luke scrambled to his feet and came in again like a charging bull. The two of them went down. Edward was first on his feet. Jassy caught his arm. Luke took his chance, and before Edward could free himself had sent him heavily into the wall. He slid down, apparently stunned.

Luke said: 'Jassy, I'm taking you back.'

'No.'

'What do you know of him?'

'I love him.'

'I won't let him take you away. I . . . we need you at home.'

Edward reared groggily to his feet.

'Please don't fight,' Jassy implored.

Edward threw himself bodily at Luke. The two of them blundered right across the room, clean through the doorway and out on to the ground. Rolling and punching, they piled up into a heap at the feet of Captain Hopkins, on his unsteady way back from the inn.

Hopkins reeled back a step, and muzzily wiped his eyes. Then he let out a wild bellow.

'Lieutenant Robarts!'

'Sir?'

'I want that officer and the Firbeck man put under arrest.'

'On what charges?'

'The officer is guilty of quitting his post. Firbeck is a vagabond – an outlaw – tried to assault me in the inn – '

'Come, sir.' Luke got to his feet, incredulous. 'We rode here together. I cannot believe – '

'Do you doubt my word?' Hopkins shouted at Robarts.

'I would accept it more readily, sir, if I were certain you were sober. It will be better if we discuss this in the morning.'

Jassy took out a handkerchief and dabbed at a gash of blood down Edward's jaw. He tried to intervene, making a movement of protest towards Hopkins; but the captain, bleak and menacing, was in no mood to be deflected.

'When I get to Sydney, sir' – he thrust his bulging head towards Robarts – 'I shall have much to say about this command. I've made some notes during my survey. Very many notes. Listing areas infested with vagabonds and rogues of every description. You allow squatters to run riot in Crown lands, you let them roam even within the precincts of His Majesty's prison. There is a brothel – yes, sir, a brothel within sight of the gates here. And not a moment ago an insubordinate officer was rolling out of your office and upon the ground in combat. What do you say to that, sir?'

'You make it sound more serious than it is,' said Lieutenant Robarts stiffly.

'Indeed, no. My report will make good reading – good, if not incredible. Goodnight to you.'

Jassy looked wretchedly from one young officer to another. Then looked about for Luke, in the hope of still, after all that had happened, effecting a truce and the beginning of understanding. But Luke had gone.

He sat, unmoving, at a table under a guttering tallow lamp. Moll had closed the doors, and a thin blonde girl was scrubbing the counter. Rosie, her shoulders draped in a red shawl whose flame turned her long lank hair to charcoal, glanced again and again at him; but with dwindling hope.

Jassy and Edward Elliott would be together now, in the quarters Lieutenant Robarts had offered them.

Luke came to life. He slammed the table with his fist and got up. Rosie smiled and stretched a leg across his path. He stepped over it and went to the side door leading to the veranda.

Recognizing voices from the back of the building, he was reminded of the first occasion on which he had set foot in this place. It seemed a lifetime ago. But the tenor of the argument had not changed to any great extent.

'The room is for fleas, madam.' Captain Hopkins spoke with slurred self-pity.

'If you don't like it you'd best seek elsewhere.' Moll was raucous with easily summoned indignation.

'Disgusting. That young feller finds Elliott accommodation, I notice. And me a senior officer. Just because he has a lady to keep him warm.'

Luke felt a pang in his chest. He leaned against the wall.

'Perhaps if you weren't alone,' said Moll, 'the room would seem better.'

'Eh? What?'

'Someone for company. Someone you like.'

'Rosie?' whined Hopkins hopefully.

'I'm not saying it couldn't be arranged.'

Sickened, Luke went back into the bar. Anna had arrived in his absence, looking agitated. Something must certainly have disturbed her: she seldom risked her father's wrath by crossing the street to the inn. She began to say something, but he waved her aside. He could not listen, had nothing to say to anyone. Had the strength neither to stay nor to go. He felt battered and beaten by something far more terrible than Lieutenant Elliott's fists.

Moll came in and winked at Rosie, jerking a thumb towards the door. Before the girl could hurry away, Anna said: 'I've heard something. I think you ought to know.'

The three women put their heads together. At one stage Moll let out a squawk, then growled like a cat quivering over a pigeon.

'You're sure?'

'*Heard* it. Heard him threatening. We don't want, none of us want . . .'

The words dripped meaninglessly over Luke's head. At the same moment there began a faint patter of rain on the roof of the inn. The volume increased to a steady drum-roll.

Moll slapped her knee. 'Right.'

Anna took off her necklace and passed it to Rosie. Rosie held it up to the light for a moment, then slid it with sensual satisfaction down her bodice. Now she made for the door.

Suddenly Luke wanted nothing more than to stand in the rain, to let it wash over him and drown him and carry him away. He got up, brushed past Moll and Anna, and went out into the street. But there was no refreshment in the downpour. The rain was warm. Dusty ruts in the roadway melted into mud.

Picking her way through the runnels, Jassy came towards him from the barracks. He splashed his way jubilantly to meet her.

'Jass, I knew you'd come. I waited. I wanted you to come, and I'd almost given up hope, but – '

'No, Luke.'

'We'll go home in the morning. I knew if I waited – '

'Luke, I've come to say goodbye. To make quite sure you understand it's goodbye.'

'No.'

'I must.'

'You love me.'

'No. I needed you. Needed your strength.'

'And I yours,' he said eagerly. He folded her in his arms, drew her under an awning out of the rain.

'I have none to give. You asked too much of me, and I

cannot give it to you.' She clutched his eager hand and thrust it away. 'Let me go.'

'Never. We need each other. You've said so.'

'I need love,' she said. 'I need comfort. I need children.'

'I won't let you go. How could I be sure – '

'We shall not be too far away. Edward has influence, he fancies he may be able to take over the command here. William Robarts is happy to contemplate a return to Sydney.'

'It is all to be so neat?' he cried. 'You have it all worked out, and you think it is such a pretty little substitute for what *I* have given you?'

'Luke.' She was desperate. 'I need you to set me free. Don't you see? I need your blessing.'

At last he released her. 'All I've worked for, all I've dreamed. You in your kingdom.'

'Limping, childless, in a desert.'

'Is that all it meant?'

'I'm a woman.'

'A girl.'

'A woman. Perhaps I already carry his baby.' She raised her head, and in a leaping memory which crossed her eyes he saw how wrong he had been: she was indeed a woman now.

It was over. He knew it. Utterly defeated, he knew that he could not touch her again and must not let himself think of her as he had so dangerously thought these last days. Slowly, with an infinite effort, he nodded. She let herself sink against him once more, and kissed him. He hugged her. It was as it had all been, once upon a time.

She turned away, back towards the barracks. He was about to offer her his arm and escort her round the puddles when uproar broke out, as sudden and torrential as the rain.

'Thief!' Anna was howling, as if in an endeavour to prove

that she could out-do her mother when circumstances warranted. 'My necklace! Thief!'

'I never touched your necklace.'

Hopkins erupted from the front door of the inn, trying to button up his jacket and hold his trousers up at the same time.

'Get the lieutenant, call out the guard.' Moll added her strident tones to the tumult.

A light appeared in the window of the store. Helmich came out on the steps, and Anna ran to him.

'Father, he stole my necklace.'

'It's a lie.'

Hopkins summoned what dignity he could and began to march towards the barracks. A trooper was heading down towards him, with Lieutenant Robarts a few paces behind.

'You call my daughter a liar?' screeched Moll. 'I'll give you liar, you debauched old rogue.'

Robarts and Hopkins met. Hopkins said: 'These insults must be quieted at once. Law and order must be restored to this damned place. If not – '

'Ask Rosie,' said Moll. 'Ask Rosie whether he's debauched or not. And ask her where she found my daughter's necklace.'

'Rosie, eh?' Robarts drew himself up and stared down on Hopkins's perspiring brow, growing wetter than ever in the downpour. 'Here's some fine reading for the gentlemen in Sydney.'

'I assure you, sir, there is no foundation whatsoever for – '

'Arrest him!' shouted the storekeeper. 'He should set an example. Or you should make of him an example, yes?'

'Yes,' said Robarts amiably. 'We'll discuss it in the morning. Eh, Captain Hopkins?'

'What? Eh? Oh, yes,' mumbled Hopkins, dazed. 'Yes, in the morning.'

In the morning Luke rode back the way he had come. He

rode unseeing, knowing his way by instinct. Anna had tried to persuade him to stay, offering wistful hints about the different future there would have to be, now that Jassy was gone. Moll had brazenly offered him the pick of her girls and enough drink to keep him numbed for a few days, until the fever had died. But he wanted nobody. And if he craved forgetfulness, it was not to be found through liquor.

The closer he drew to the homestead, the slower his horse's pace. Unconsciously he was holding it back. There was nothing to speed home for. Nobody there. Nothing but a great emptiness.

Last night's rain had swollen the little streams below the track. In one or two places were shallow lakes, fast disappearing.

On the edge of one tract of water a group of aborigines had assembled. He heard them chattering happily enough as he approached, but when he came in sight they were silent, watching him, making no move to address him or to leave.

They were on Firbeck land. They ought to be driven off. But not now. Later he would summon up the energy to do all the usual things that needed doing.

A girl bent over the water, cupping her hands and pouring it over her head and shoulders. Through his indifference he was aware of her movements, and remained aware of them long after he had ridden past.

Black velvet.

He quickened his pace now, until he was within half a mile of the homestead. From this crest he could see the proud beacon of their stone chimney.

After a moment's contemplation he turned away, the taste of nausea in his mouth mingling with a sour, savage desire which had to be slaked.

CHAPTER EIGHT

On 23rd April 1832 Jason Firbeck, attired in a new suit and sporting a bright new silk cravat, was driven by his son-in-law to Government House in Sydney. The suit had been made by Helmich the storekeeper from a smart London pattern not more than twelve months old. Jason intended to show the administrators that a squatter was not necessarily a vagrant. And there would be words to match. As the sulky clipped along at a fine pace, he silently rehearsed for the hundredth time the points he must lay before the Governor's Commission.

Samuel rode behind, maintaining a gap of some ten to fifteen yards. He was enjoying the excursion. Luke had shown no wish to take his place. Very much the opposite: governors, judges, magistrates and all other officers of the Crown belonged to a class, he was convinced, intent only on retaining their own privileges even if that meant ripping the clothes from the backs of the less privileged – and smart new clothes would fare no better than old rags and tatters.

Jason had been discovering bit by bit that young Edward Elliott was a man of more influence than one would have suspected from his shy, gentle demeanour. The transfer of the Kinbone village command had been swiftly accomplished, and Edward and Jassy were installed there within a matter of weeks. Now, they had hardly set foot in Government House before Governor Bourke himself was greeting the young lieutenant.

'What's this I hear, my boy? Got yourself married, settled back of beyond?'

'Perfectly true, sir.'

'Some comely filly, I trust. Anyone I know?'

'May I introduce her father, sir – '

'Your servant, Excellency,' said Jason with a stiff bow.

'Jason Firbeck,' said Edward.

'Firbeck . . . Firbeck . . . ?'

'A squatter, Excellency,' said Edward.

Bourke raised bushy white eyebrows in some amazement, then burst out laughing. 'Might have known you'd be up to something. Going to knock some sense into that Committee of mine, eh?' Apparently on impulse he handed Jason a folded newspaper. 'I've been letting the papers have more freedom since I took over here, y'know. See what they make of it.'

He exchanged a few civilities with Edward, and then Jason was shown to an ante-room to await his turn to give evidence before the Commission of Inquiry. He soon found the passage to which the Governor must have been referring. Perhaps it would have been better if he had failed to do so. By the time he was ushered into the committee room he was in such a rage that all his finest phrases and reasoned arguments had been banished from his head. He brandished the crumpled newspaper like a sabre.

'I have come all this way to find such slanders being uttered against our community? I am asked to give testimony to a supposedly impartial court when no check is placed on the circulation of pernicious lies?'

The chairman, a magistrate with a beaked nose and a habit of dabbing his tongue petulantly between his lips when he wished to express disapproval, tapped the table for silence.

'Mr – ah – Firbeck, this will not do. By what right do you address us so intemperately? If you are angry – '

'Angry?' exploded Jason. 'Have I not grounds for anger?' He opened out the offending sheet and read in a trembling voice: ' "The squatters" – the writer is referring to *us*, sir – "the squatters are a great public grievance. Continued delay in eradicating them will not be countenanced by the substantial citizens of this land. Rumours of leniency and of proposed accommodations with such vagabonds must be scotched forthwith if the new administration is to command respect throughout the colony." A public grievance!' Jason echoed. 'A grievance, if you please, upon which the colony grows rich – '

'The view of a journalist, Mr Firbeck,' said the magistrate irritably.

'A view not confined to the pages of this rag. What grievance can be held against men improving the land? We do so entirely at our own risk, sir. We are left to bargain with neighbours for the boundaries of our pastures, left to build roadways and drains, defend our stock, indeed our very families.' He stared accusingly at the uniformed figure of the officer who had already been introduced as Major Harwood, regional military commandant. Harwood had not even joined the other members of the committee at the table, but stood by the window, his back half turned. 'Defend ourselves,' Jason flung at him, 'from the ravages of blacks and runaways, *and* from your escaped villains, sir – brutalized, hungry, without respect for the sanctity of life and possessions.' He took a deep breath, and looked away, catching a gently warning glance from Edward Elliott at the back of the room. 'We are condemned, sir,' he went on to the magistrate, 'as outlaws. To live as they do, by wit and cunning. Is it a grievance, sir, that we demand our rights, as free people in an English land, to security and protection?'

Harwood moved indolently away from the window and rested his fingertips on the end of the table. 'Demand is it?' he said softly. 'You are right, sir. There *are* adverse opinions. And within these very walls, and no shame on that. Opinions that by taking livestock, supplies and wagons beyond the official limits you and your kind have created a habitable refuge for the runaways you complain of, where before there was none. Opinions that by occupying vast areas of land you have aggravated the aboriginal and turned him against us. Are you not aware, sir, that the whole border is smouldering? We could well be on the brink of war.'

Jason observed that Edward, sadly pursing his lips, was quietly leaving the committee room.

'Our duty lies, gentlemen' – Harwood had turned his attention to the other members of the committee – 'with the preservation of the official borders, not with their erosion. We cannot disperse what little strength we have for the benefit of a handful of opportunists squatting beyond the precincts of the law.'

Another witness began to protest, but was ordered by the magistrate to wait his turn. A prosperous-looking man in a frock coat who began to speak loudly and immoderately in support of Major Harwood was not so promptly suppressed.

Jason sat down and dismally twisted the newspaper between his palms. He could only hope that Samuel was making better use of his time.

The Female Factory in Parramatta made a show of living up to its original concept as a centre of reform and rehabilitation by the provision of looms and a constant supply of wool. Reports sent home to England emphasized its financial benefit to the community and the moral benefit to the women workers. Application to the simple processes of carding and spinning could lead to further skills, reborn pride, and the eventual restoration of a cleansed and reinvigorated human being to society.

Although he had learned to treat all official pronouncements in this country with some scepticism, Samuel had not yet become as bitterly disenchanted as his brother. He was quite unprepared for what met his eyes when the door to the main workroom was thrown open. His eyes – and his nose.

The stench was appalling. The vision no less hellish. No savage cartoonist of the scurrilous London journals could have done justice to this reeking bedlam. Here were the dregs of womanhood: bedraggled, filthy, noisome, with bared yellow teeth or too often, no teeth at all, clustering round bales of wool to spit jokes and abuse at each other, caterwauling and cursing while children clung to their skirts and learned the same words and the same ways.

And it was here he had come to choose a clean, wholesome, upright servant, a girl fit to take Jassy's place in their household.

'You'd do best looking elsewhere.' The factory supervisor, her square face hardened against all horror or compassion, rattled her keys and stood back to let him out again. 'These are . . . *used* . . . if you take my meaning. None of 'em fit for the wife of a gentleman.'

'I am not seeking a wife.' Samuel grasped the official permit Edward Elliott had obtained for him from the Governor. 'I need a servant.'

The woman shrugged and clicked her fingers. An elderly convict carrying a whip stepped forward.

'Connelly will accompany you.'

'I need no guard, thank you.'

She laughed. 'I'm a better judge of that, I fancy.'

Samuel forced himself to move forward, down the centre of the factory floor. His appearance was the signal for a wild outcry of jeering and cackling. A few children began to cry. Hands clawed out at Samuel's coat.

'Pick me, sir.'

'Keep your bed warm, mister?'

'I may not be beautiful, but nobody never said – '

Connelly's whip lashed the hands aside.

'I'm innocent . . . please . . . they've no right to keep me in here . . .'

Connelly's elbow toppled her over against the hard edge of a loom.

'Grog, sir? I could fancy a nice nip o' grog.'

Samuel paced on through the nightmare. There could, in God's name, be no answer here. But there was none outside: women were scarce, and labour freely given by well-trained girls almost impossible to come by. He felt engulfed by a rising tide of pleading faces, leering faces, mocking and tragic and grotesque faces.

All at once there was a quite different face immediately before him. A uniformed man with a black patch over his eye stood surveying the chaos of the room, flanked by a clergyman and an armed trooper.

The supervisor bustled past Samuel and dropped a quick curtsy. 'Begging your pardon, sir, I didn't know you was here.'

'I want to be sure this place bears some semblance of industry, Mrs Widdicombe. His Excellency the Governor comes from Sydney three days hence. He may wish to visit us. We want to make a good impression, don't we?'

'Yes, sir.'

'A *well-disciplined* impression.'

'Yes, sir.'

The man looked Samuel up and down as if to demand his business and then, evidently recognizing the nature of the official document he was carrying, said offhandedly: 'In search of a bargain, sir? You'll find only dregs here, I regret to say.'

He swept on his way, with the clergyman scuttling in attendance.

Samuel closed his eyes for a moment. When he opened them, the scene had not changed. He moved away from the middle of the room, fearing he would make a fool of himself if he did not have the support of a wall to lean on.

He stopped by a heavy door with a small grille. As he glanced in, not from curiosity but simply from the need to have some respite from the madhouse behind him, he found a bright pair of eyes staring back at him – wild eyes, like those of a cat. Then they went dark. Either the lids had closed over them, or the creature had darted for cover.

'Who's in there?' he asked.

'Oh, that one, sir.' The supervisor came back from ushering her unexpected visitors down the room. 'A viper, sir. No good'll ever come out of that, sir.'

'Viper's right,' Connelly agreed. 'You saw the Surgeon-General's eye.'

'Surgeon-General?'

'Him what just went through. What's under that patch of his – or rather, what ain't under it no more – that was her doin'.'

Samuel hesitated, then said: 'Open up this cell.'

Connelly mutely consulted the supervisor. She shook her head. 'Orders are, no one's to go near her.'

Samuel extended his permit. 'Do local orders override the Lieutenant-Governor of the colony?'

'It'll mean nothing but trouble.'

But Connelly opened the door.

Samuel advanced cautiously into the foetid little box of a room. The girl crouched against the far wall, her arms and legs tangled in terror. She must have been starved close to death, yet there was beauty in every line of her – a wild cat, perhaps, but exquisite as only a cat can be. He remembered, as a child, seeing caged birds once in England, and being horrified and dreaming helplessly of them for long after; and knew he would dream again, ten times worse, if he left this trapped, tormented creature in this bondage.

'What's her name?'

'Kate,' said Connelly. 'Kate Bell.'

Samuel went down on his haunches and held out one hand, a few inches from her. 'Kate. Would you like to be out of here?'

She concentrated not on his face but on his hand, as if summoning up the will to strike.

'The Surgeon-General's not a man to be trifled with, sir.' The supervisor sounded, in her way, as scared as Kate looked. 'You'd best let me show you one of the dormitories. Find someone a bit better suited.'

He ignored her. Against the rise and fall of hideous background clamour he coaxed the girl with the gentle sound of his voice rather than the words themselves. 'You want to be away from this hell, Kate? You'd like to come and live with us? You would: I know it. With me and my father and my brother – be a sister to us, walk in grasses under the deep blue of the sky. You'll have a home, you'll bake for us and care for us. And we'll care for you. No one in the world shall harm you. Will you come, Kate?'

Her fingers crooked, nails poised to slash at anyone who dared to mock her.

'This won't do,' said Mrs Widdicombe. 'You can't take this one, you really can't.'

'*Any* inmate of my choice.' Samuel backed away, cajoling Kate towards the cell doorway. 'That's what my permit says.'

There was a sudden breathless hush in the workroom as Kate emerged on all fours. She sniffed around like an apprehensive animal, then got unsteadily to her feet. Samuel put out a hand to steady her, but she flinched and dabbed him away.

'You'll regret it, sir. Have no doubt.' And to Kate the supervisor added maliciously: 'You'll be back.'

Samuel shouldered his way through the awestruck crowd of women. Kate followed, tottering from side to side, her hand flailing for support from each loom she passed. Still she would not accept the offer of his arm.

When they stepped out into the yard, into the cool tang of the evening air, he feared for a moment that she might collapse. For the first time she looked straight at him, needing to trust but incapable yet of trusting anyone.

Connelly had followed them down. He nudged Samuel's arm with a certain comradely admiration, and indicated they should go into an office beside the entrance gate.

'Have to enter up the details from that permit of yours.' He lifted a ledger down from a shelf.

Samuel said: 'How long has she been in here?'

'A year.'

'What did she do?'

'They don't often bother to tell us.' Connelly found a page in the register and ran a grubby finger down it. 'Bell, Kate. Convicted Finchley, 11th January 1831. Released into custody of . . . ?' He looked up.

'Samuel Firbeck.'

Connelly wrote the name painstakingly.

'And why should there be all this concern about the Surgeon-General?'

'Ah. That one. He was surgeon on that prison ship for a start, on his way out here. He fancied her. Or so they say. That's how it works: first pick to officers, then non-commissioned, then the soldiers. The likes o' me gets what's left. Well, him, he tried a liberty, and she clawed his face. That eye jumped out of its socket like an egg from the hen, so I've heard.'

'And he wants to keep her locked away for ever, just to – '

'Had her flogged. Twenty-five, then fifty. Since she came here she's had fifty regular. I've carried her back meself, with blood spurtin' from what was left of her shoes where she walked, an' ants carryin' away pieces of her. And after that he'd . . . well, he'd fancy her very special.'

Samuel turned away to hide what must surely be in his face.

Kate stood rapt in the doorway, gazing out at the sunset flooding resplendently up above the rooftops.

Out in the road a chain gang shuffled back to prison. Some twenty men carried two huge beams, followed by a corporal and two soldiers taking their ease in a bullock cart.

'Six months he's had her shut away in there,' said Connelly placidly. 'Keep her out of temptation, he says.'

There was a shout from outside. 'What ho, me little beauty. Now there's a beauty, 'pon my oath.'

All at once the doorway was empty. Kate had slipped away without a sound. As Samuel strode towards the opening, the corporal swaggered past. 'Hey, not goin' to say no to a bit o' sport, are we?'

Samuel sprang out of the office.

'The permit,' Connelly shouted after him. 'You'll need your permit with you.'

A soldier stood by the railings with hands on hips, laughing, as the corporal broke into a run after Kate. She took to her heels and was out of the gate and into the road in a flash. The second man saw her coming and dropped from the cart into her path. She shot to one side and round the corner of a building.

'Kate! Don't run! I'll be with you!'

Samuel turned back to grab his horse's bridle. They raced out of the gate. A trooper raised his musket. Samuel reared his horse and kicked the man in the face. Then he was galloping down the alley and out across a patch of waste ground with open country beyond.

There was no sign of Kate in the flush of deepening twilight. Desperately he wheeled round; saw only the straggling outskirts of the town; and went round again.

Her only possible concealment was in a wedge of gum trees widening away from the river towards the hills.

'Kate!'

Branches snatched at his face and arms as he rode into

the wood. The undergrowth thickened. He would soon be brought down in the darkness if he tried to force his way through on horseback. Dismounting, he stood quite still for a moment. And heard, some way ahead, the crashing and rustling of a wild creature throwing herself madly through all obstacles.

He kicked his way on until he saw the trail she had made for herself. A few hundred yards farther, and he heard her sobbing and panting helplessly.

At last she was there, a frail shadow in the gloom, trying to summon a last effort to flee. He threw himself forward. She went down in a heap, her head on her knees.

'Kate.' He approached warily and touched her shoulder. She writhed away. 'Kate, it's over. You needn't have been frightened. You're free. Don't you understand? Free.'

Slowly she got to her feet. He pointed back along the swathe the two of them had trampled through the undergrowth.

'We'll collect my horse,' he said in a tone as level and reassuring as he could make it, 'and camp here. Try to get some sleep. Tomorrow we'll go home. Home,' he said warmly, letting the sound and the idea of it sink into her doubting, fearful mind.

Kate rode in the dawn towards the Blue Mountains, the prison wall beyond which lay liberty. Samuel walked beside the horse. He had tried to persuade her to sit in front of him, but she still shied away from such close contact. For a while he would have to humour her, though it meant the journey would take that much longer. And he was anxious to be up through the canyons as soon as possible, to put behind them this land which smelt so rankly of evil, and reach the security of their kingdom.

The call of a bell bird drew them to a watercourse, and they stopped to drink. Scooping up water and watching the droplets splash over her arms, Kate ventured a smile. The breath caught in Samuel's throat. He saw the true intimations of the beauty she must have had once, the beauty which could so easily be restored.

They had been on the move again for less than twenty minutes when the ominous sound of racing hoofbeats came up behind them. Samuel led the horse to one side of the track in the hope that the riders would pass.

They did not pass, but reined in. The corporal was unmistakably the one who had scared Kate the evening before. His two troopers rode in on either side of Samuel.

'Don't be afraid.' Samuel looked commandingly up at Kate.

The corporal said: 'You'll hang for this.'

'For what?'

'Aiding an escaped convict.'

'She's an assigned servant.'

'Assigned? To a vagabond?'

'Keep a civil tongue in your head, or it'll be the worse for you. I'm a free settler.'

'Let's see your papers.'

'You very well know we have no such things.'

'Hers, then.' The corporal licked his lower lip appreciatively. 'There'd have to be papers for *her*.'

'I . . .' He realized, with a chill, where he had left the document in his haste to find Kate and calm her. 'The official warrant is still in Parramatta. That man Connelly, at the Female Factory – he'll still have it. He was entering up the particulars.'

'I doubt that,' said the corporal. 'Oh, I doubt very much if Connelly will know anything about it. Or that there'll be any particulars.' He advanced on Kate. 'You'd best be coming with me.'

She slid from the horse in terror. One of the troopers dropped beside her and encircled her waist with his arm.

Her head wrenched back, she twisted in his grip, and her right hand stabbed twice, her nails scoring deeply into his cheek.

He yelled. The corporal laughed. Samuel leapt forward, but the second trooper leaned over and struck him down with the butt of his musket. Now the corporal, taking the precaution of using both arms, grabbed Kate from behind and lifted her bodily off the ground.

'Tie her legs.'

'I'll have you flogged.' Samuel lurched to his knees. 'Your superiors will hear of this.'

'My superiors have already heard. Would I be here otherwise? There's a certain gentleman wants his hell-cat back – for reasons best known to himself.'

'I'm a free settler – '

'And you'll dangle from a gibbet as pretty as the next,' said the corporal with relish. 'Now, let's be taking you both where you belong.'

CHAPTER NINE

The name of Firbeck carried no weight in Parramatta gaol. Few names meant anything there. 'I tell you I'm Samuel Firbeck, and my father Jason Firbeck has been appearing before the Governor's Commission. I insist that word is conveyed to him . . .' It met with scorn or indifference. 'A few years in here'll cure anyone of worrying about who they used to be,' said one guard. 'Surprising the number as forgets their names altogether.' The idea of a prisoner being allowed to send a message to Government House was laughable. The system did not work that way. Messages travelled downwards, not upwards.

But the name of Firbeck did, after a day or so, strike a resonance.

Major Harwood, inspecting the barracks and prison in anticipation of the Governor's forthcoming visit, said: 'Firbeck? I'd no idea he was in Parramatta. You've detained Firbeck?'

'S'what he said.'

'Corporal – '

'Bailey, sir,' said the man ingratiatingly. 'Corporal Bailey.'

'I'm not especially interested in *your* name, man. But Firbeck, you said? Detained – on what charge?'

'Helping an escaped convict, sir. A woman.'

'Not my old friend Surgeon Hall's . . . ?'

'That's the one, sir.'

Harwood struck his forehead wonderingly. 'Jason Firbeck abducting a female convict!'

'Beggin' your pardon, sir. His name's Samuel.'

Harwood contemplated the guardroom wall for a long moment. Then he turned his gaze on Corporal Bailey.

'I do not think his name is Samuel.'

'He's been clear enough on that score, making no end of a commotion about – '

'You have not heard the name Samuel. And you'll say nothing of all this, d'you hear? Nothing to anyone. Just have the girl sent along to my quarters right away.'

'But sir – '

'Do as I tell you.'

Bailey saluted and left the room. When he had gone, Harwood leafed through the official report sheets until he found the appropriate one, withdrew it from under the duty sergeant's nose, and screwed it up.

'The Firbecks,' he said venomously. 'A family of incorrigible trouble-makers.'

The Firbecks: one of them dining with the Governor and in return feeding him with subversive proposals which must inevitably lead to the collapse of all discipline in the colony; the other lying with his fellow rats in gaol! Gaol was where both of them belonged. The whole tribe, damn it, and hundreds more like them. Flooding westwards over land which should be reserved for legitimate claimants. Recognize squatters like the Firbecks and you rewarded them for breaking the law. Harbouring convicts, enticing labour from the eastern settlements, selling grog on the sly, corrupting the army and harassing its patrols, inflaming the enmity of the aborigines – how could they be checked other than by the sternest repression? The previous Governor had held out against compromise with such outlaws, until his position was undermined by traitors who forced his recall and shamefully tried to bring about his impeachment. That was the reward for integrity and discipline! The new man was a waverer, a weakling. His nose would have to be rubbed in some harsh facts.

And if the facts were not vivid enough, there was no harm in colouring them slightly to achieve the best effect.

Harwood stood before the mantelpiece of his study, surveying his guests with an air of satisfaction which made the Reverend Amos Pilcher uneasy and Surgeon-General Hall downright impatient.

'We have been plagued,' said Harwood at last, 'by the insistence of the man Firbeck. He has insinuated himself into the counsels of the Governor, he seems to have won His Excellency's ear, no attempt is made to curb him – '

'I cannot accept that.' The magistrate bristled. 'I allowed him as little leeway as possible at the hearings.'

'You did what you could, Mr Bretherington,' Harwood conceded. 'It was not enough. But now I think we may have in our grasp a means of lowering His Excellency's opinion of this rogue.' He savoured the pause, then said: 'There is today lodged against him a grave charge, gentlemen. Immorality. Indecency. Abduction.'

Bretherington gaped. 'I confess I was not drawn to the fellow, but even so I should scarce have thought – '

'We can destroy Firbeck. I think it essential that we do so without delay. It would be a long time before another such would dare show his face in Government House.'

Harwood rang a small bell on the mantelpiece close to his elbow.

The door opened. Kate Bell was led in by a sergeant. She stood blinking, petrified, in the lamplight. Surgeon-General Hall beamed at her and purred a welcome.

'I think, Surgeon Hall,' said Harwood, 'that you should have the pleasure of laying the formal charges. I know you feel a personal interest in the welfare of this poor girl. Now, my child.' He turned to Kate. 'You have had a distressing experience. You have been guilty of some deplorable mistakes, but all of us here are willing to believe that you were more sinned against than sinning. There is to be an inquiry into your shameful maltreatment. If you speak the truth, the court will view your attempt at escape with leniency. We wish only to help you. You promise to speak the truth?'

Kate's lips worked, but no sound came out.

'You will be asked questions in court,' said Harwood with heavy patience. 'All you have to do is answer them clearly. Answer them as you know they must be answered. When the time comes you will know what the answers must be, of that I'm sure.'

Four magistrates occupied the bench in the Parramatta courtroom. As well as Bretherington and the Reverend Amos Pilcher there were a younger magistrate named McKie and a landowner, Bartlett. All respected members of the community who knew where their consciences lay. Major Harwood felt safe in their hands. They each greeted him and Surgeon-General Hall with grave courtesy, and Bretherington invited the Surgeon-General to state the charge they were to consider.

The black patch seemed to burn more intensely than Hall's remaining good eye. Righteous indignation oozed from it.

'As you know, gentlemen, it is my bounden duty to watch over the interests of the female workers entrusted to my care. If a prisoner proves a danger to society, I am not lax in chastisement.' The magistrates nodded sober approval. 'But where a prisoner capable of reform can be allowed some latitude, I allow it. And if she should from time to time make a perfectly human error of judgement, I am capable of forgiveness. Our whole system preaches forgiveness and reformation. *But*' – Hall raised one admonitory finger majestically – 'when attempts to reform a wretched transgressor are perverted by the uncontrolled appetites of some so-called *free settler*, taking both the law and a woman's shrinking body into his own hands . . . then I feel it is my duty to lay the facts of such criminality before this court and the entire community, so that such evil influence may be curbed without delay.'

'This court accepts your motives, Surgeon Hall,' said Bretherington amiably. 'Will you now please name the parties concerned?'

'I have to report that a prisoner, Kate Bell, foolishly attempting an escape from the Parramatta Female Factory, where she had been shown nothing but kindness and consideration, was callously misled and assaulted by a squatter returning from Sydney through the Parramatta region. An attempt was made to abduct the unfortunate girl beyond the borders of the Nineteen Counties. This was foiled, I'm relieved to say, by the alertness of one of Major Harwood's patrols. The name of the debaucher of defenceless womanhood I declare to be Jason Firbeck.'

Hall stood down.

Bretherington turned to Harwood. 'I believe you have a submission to make, Major Harwood.'

'Thank you, sir. The first and principle witness is a non-commissioned officer for whose character and sense of duty I can vouch.'

Corporal Bailey was led into the well of the court by a young lieutenant.

'A man of excellent character,' Harwood stressed, 'who has been with the Service eleven years, and in that time has not been convicted of perjury or any disrespect to a court of law.'

McKie leaned over the bench. 'Perhaps you will tell us in your own words what happened.'

'Yes, sir. Your honour, sir. I was patrolling, an' I come upon the Firbeck gentleman an' the lady. It being several miles from habitation, an' early in the mornin', I concluded they'd passed the night in . . . well, you might say in each other's company. Beggin' your pardon, sir.'

There was a long pause. McKie frowned. 'Yes? Is that all?'

The corporal looked blank, and risked an apprehensive glance at his commanding officer. Harwood prompted: 'The action you then took . . . ?'

'Oh, oh yes. Naturally I apprehended him.'

'And the name of the man you apprehended – you're quite sure of it?'

'Quite sure, sir.' Corporal Bailey brightened. He had rehearsed this bit well enough. 'Mr Firbeck, sir.'

'And the lady,' interposed Surgeon Hall, 'was a convict girl – '

'Yes, sir.'

'Helpless at the mercy of the man Firbeck.'

Bailey again looked unsure of himself. Harwood, with a menacing edge to his voice, urged: 'The girl thus saved made a complaint to you?' When the corporal still wavered, Harwood deemed it safer to hurry on. 'If I may save the court's time. She told the corporal that Firbeck had interfered with her, threatened her, made improper suggestions and unwelcome advances – which she resisted, I may add, with courage and honour.'

'And that is the case?' McKie appeared far from happy. He looked around the courtroom. 'This Mr Firbeck – is he present?'

'I fear not,' said Harwood.

'But since he is in custody, surely he should have the right to hear the serious charges brought against him.'

Harwood nodded to the lieutenant and the corporal, dismissing them from the hearing. As McKie was about to object to this highhandedness, Harwood said quickly: 'I crave the court's indulgence. Firbeck's innate violence was not as immediately apparent to the patrol as it was to those of us who have seen him haranguing the Governor's Commission. He contrived to escape. I have severely disciplined the corporal and his men – regretfully, for I have already given you my high opinion of Corporal Bailey. But I would not wish him to undergo further humiliation by having to listen to the story again before this court.'

'Firbeck was apprehended – and escaped? May we take it that a warrant has been issued for his immediate pursuit and arrest?'

'By now, sir,' said Harwood stiffly, 'we may be sure he is across the limits and back with his fellow outlaws – beyond our jurisdiction.'

The sulky rolled smartly down the far from smart village street. Jason leaned back and patted his stomach. He was well fed and well disposed towards the world. His spell in the city had given him a new perspective on shabby outposts such as this, and at the same time an unexpected new affection for it. He grinned at Moll as she waved a jug of ale over a road gang working as vainly as ever to make the thoroughfare less of a quagmire. She screeched a welcome at him. And her daughter Anna ran from the store towards the carriage as it bumped gently to a halt.

'Mr Firbeck, we've missed you. Lieutenant Elliott.'

'My, my,' said Jason expansively. 'Anna, if you're not the first pretty face I've seen this three weeks and more.'

'You're teasing, Mr Firbeck.'

'Edward, did I not say how lacking in grace were the ladies in Sydney?'

'You also had some things to say about the men,' observed Edward dryly. He turned to smile up the street as Jassy came running from the barracks, her skirts gathered up clear of the dust – running gracefully, not too fast, but with an eagerness that touched her father's heart.

'And Parramatta?' said Anna. 'I'm told there are rather

more ladies – of one kind and another – in Parramatta than there are in Sydney.'

'Oh, I left that to Samuel. Doubtless he'll already have given you his views.'

Jassy reached them and indulged herself in a gentle, lingering kiss with Edward, while Anna watched enviously.

'Samuel?' said Anna, only half attentive. 'Isn't he with you?'

Jason looked perturbed. 'You mean you haven't seen him? But he should have been here well ahead of us. We hardly expected to catch him up, if he rode straight back from Parramatta – but I assumed that by now . . .'

'He's probably found other diversions.' Jassy linked her arm in her husband's. 'Come home and tell me all about your trip.'

'No, come in and tell *us* all about it.' Anna coaxed. 'We hear so little. Father's so interested in what the Governor would make of your depositions.'

'Well . . .' Jason looked uneasily back up the trail as if at any moment, on some signal, Samuel would appear.

'I shall go back,' said Edward.

Jassy's consternation was touching and laughable. 'You will do no such thing. Please, no. Samuel can look after himself. Perhaps later . . . you can ride part of the way to meet him. But now, please . . .'

'Let us hear what life is like in the cities,' begged Anna.

McKie said: 'And the convict girl – is *she* here?'

Kate Bell was led into court. The lieutenant had virtually to guide her round the ends of the benches: she seemed incapable of opening her eyes.

'There's nothing to be afraid of, my dear.' Mr Pilcher held out one pale hand in vague benediction.

She took the oath in a lifeless monotone.

'Now.' Bretherington was determined to have the ritual

briskly over and done with. 'Tell us about this Firbeck man.

Kate opened her eyes and darted a green, feline gaze from one face to the other. Then the eyes seemed to cloud over again.

'Speak up, my dear,' said Surgeon Hall, lethally gentle. 'Speak up and say what you have to say.' When there was no response, he did not alter his tone. 'You do confirm that the man *was* Firbeck?'

'I heard it said, yes.'

'Before he assaulted you, or – '

'He . . . he gave me no cause but to be grateful to him,' Kate blurted out. And was utterly still.

Harwood's heel scraped discordantly on the floor.

McKie glanced dubiously at his colleagues. When none of them spoke, he addressed Kate: 'You do not say, then, that he acted improperly towards you?'

'No, sir.'

'Then I fail to see quite what case we are – '

'He is a kind man,' said Kate.

Pilcher stirred. 'You are on oath, child.'

'You complained to my corporal,' snapped Harwood.

'No.'

'What the deuce has come over you? I know the memories must be painful, but for all our sakes we must have the right answers to these questions. The *right* answers, child. Shall we start again? You told Corporal Bailey that Jason Firbeck had taken unpardonable liberties with you.'

'No.'

'Did you not tell him that Mr Firbeck forced you to comply with his wishes?'

'Never.'

'Forced you to the ground, dragged up your petticoats – '

'No.' Kate's eyes were wide open now. She stared into a future of retribution, but was not shaken. 'Mr Firbeck is a gentleman.'

The major controlled himself with difficulty. 'Do you expect the court to accept your word – the word of a transported felon – before that of a soldier serving in the army of His Majesty?'

She remained unassailable. The stubbornness that had stood her in such good stead through such a plague of terrors was all she had left. It stood up against Harwood's mounting, more and more demented harangue. Twice McKie tried to interrupt on the witness's behalf but was overruled by his three colleagues.

'Every chance to speak the truth,' Harwood raged on. 'Do you know, girl, what befalls liars before a court of law?' Shudderingly he forced himself to a lull; a last attempt at sweet reason. 'Do not be stubborn. You lodged a complaint with my corporal. You told him how you had suffered at Firbeck's uncouth hands – '

'No, sir.' Kate's voice was harsh enough to match his own. 'It was at your soldiers' hands that I suffered.'

'What? A new tale? Not enough that you should spend a night with an outlaw. Now you wish to implicate gallant serving soldiers. Perhaps you'd have us believe that you are irresistible to *all* men?'

Kate's gaze swivelled slowly upon the Surgeon-General, who shivered and looked away.

The Reverend Mr Pilcher touched his fingertips gently together. 'You wish us to believe, child, that although you spent a night alone with this man Firbeck – a passionate man, as we all know who have heard him in debate – a night alone with him . . . nothing at all took place? Nothing?'

'Upon my oath, sir.'

'Careful, child. To speak falsely on oath is to blaspheme.'

'I speak the truth.'

There was no breaking her. Bretherington took it on himself to dismiss her from the hearing before further damage could be done. He then recalled Corporal Bailey and, on the Surgeon-General's tight-lipped suggestion, the bench also heard character evidence regarding Kate Bell from Mrs Widdicombe, supervisor of the Female Factory. The character was not one which Harwood had originally planned to present: it was all the doomed girl now merited.

When the magistrates reached their conclusions it was time for the lamps to be lit. In their sour yellow glow each of them signed the statement – McKie only after some heated argument. When it was dry Bretherington read it out.

'While no charge has yet been officially served on Jason Firbeck, in his absence we find the basic facts proven. If Firbeck should set foot within the Nineteen Counties at any time henceforth he shall at once be apprehended and brought for trial. As to the witness Bell . . .'

'Stand up, Kate Bell,' intoned Mr Pilcher.

'Bell,' said Bretherington solemnly, 'the bench finds you guilty of wilful and corrupt perjury. You will therefore be taken hence and committed to His Majesty's gaol and there held until an opportunity affords for your banishment to Fort Macquarie, there to remain during the full term of your natural – '

'I spoke the truth!' she cried. 'I told you the truth!'

'Take her away.'

Samuel took three paces forward and three back. He could achieve no more, and even those steps had to be kept short and cramped. Along an echoing corridor someone howled a drunken dirge, and every now and then came the sound of a woman sobbing. Little distinction was made between men's and women's accommodation in this odious place.

He put his hands against the dripping, encrusted wall. Perhaps eventually he would become like the rest – capable of drinking the very sweat of decay off the stones, of lying in his own filth and ceasing to care. Or to hope.

Already one day had proved a lifetime, two a steeply sloping entrance to hell. And tomorrow . . . ? When nobody would listen, nobody grant him the most elementary rights of every free Englishman under a supposedly incorruptible English administration, how could there ever be a ray of light?

Luke had been right. Luke, implacably savage and hating, had been right from the very beginning.

There was a clash of keys, the clang of a door. Footsteps slouched along the passage.

'But I'm innocent.' The voice dragged him away from the wall to the grating in his door. 'I was told to speak the truth, and I did nothing but speak the truth.'

'In there.'

Another crash of a door, the cruel final scrape of key in lock, and a plangent echo grinding away into the void.

Samuel thrust his face close to the bars. 'Kate?'

His voice was added to the distorted reverberations.

'I told the truth, Jason. I did tell the truth.'

Jason? It was another distortion, all part of the whole terrible nightmare.

'Kate!'

'Quiet along there,' bellowed a guard.

'My name's Samuel, Kate. Samuel Firbeck. Jason's my father. What made you – '

'Shut that man up.'

A corporal and a guard came stamping along the passage.

'What have they done to my father, then? What . . .'

His view was blocked by a drunken, twisted face he remembered all too well. It was the corporal who had dragged them back, and now gloated over the power he held.

'You bastard,' said Samuel. And spat, hard and accurately.

'Let me in. Give me that key and by God I'll show this . . . the key, you fool, the key . . .'

'What does she know about my father? What tricks have you been up to, you warped little bastard?'

'I warned you.'

Corporal Bailey wrenched the door open and staggered in, snatching the guard's musket as he came. He raised it to drive the muzzle into Samuel's face. Samuel jerked aside, grabbed the stock and pulled. The corporal crashed forward into the cell. Samuel swung the musket down towards him and cocked it, in full view of the guard outside.

'Come in here, you.' The guard wavered. 'In here,' said Samuel, 'or your friend'll get what he deserves.'

The guard advanced sullenly into the cell. Light glinted on the keys still swinging from his fingers. Samuel reached for them and backed warily away.

'Which is the girl's key?' When there was no reply, he said: 'Better order your trooper to speak, Corporal, or your head'll be no more than a great black hole.'

'Tell him,' whispered the corporal.

The guard jabbed a finger. 'That one.'

Samuel edged out of the door, both locking it and slamming the bolts behind him. He ran along the corridor. 'Kate, where are you?' Her strangled cry drew him to a cell door from which she stared out disbelieving – not daring to believe, not risking it again so soon.

He flung her door open. 'Come on. Stay close.'

He urged her along a passage to a flight of steps, down to a door which opened without trouble before them, and out into the prison courtyard. There was a steady shouting and banging from within, and a rush of footsteps. Flattening himself against the wall of the main building, Samuel crept to the corner. A trooper stood silhouetted in the doorway of the guardroom, listening, then turned and hurried back inside. Samuel put out his hand to take Kate's and draw her after him.

She was not there.

'Where *are* you . . . ?'

Her shadow fluttered against the wall, like an imprisoned moth. He seized her arm and dragged her after him, out across the yard. They had reached the shadows of a stores block just as two troopers rode in through the gateway.

'What's all that din?'

Samuel eased open a door, and they trod their way carefully through the gloom, past crates and bales towards a faint gleam of light. At the rear of the building a small lamp stood on a trestle table beside an open ledger. There was nobody there. And, as Samuel looked round in the uncertain light, there seemed to be no way out. He peered up into the rafters. High in one wall was a shuttered window.

There was a clatter of hoofs across the yard outside. Somebody barked orders, and there was an urgent bugle call.

Samuel studied the pile of sacks and boxes against the wall, and began to drag a few more sacks into position at the base. He tested the foundation with his foot and gestured to Kate that she should climb up. Shakily she obeyed. When she was halfway to the top he set off after her, his weight pressing the pile more securely to the wall.

They settled themselves close to the window. He drove the musket through glass and shutter, and waited. The noise of pursuit was fading away in the opposite direction, out of the main gateway. When he hauled himself over the sill, brushing fragments of broken glass away, it was to see a long slope of roof tilting away from the main stores building, down to a quiet lane.

Samuel eased himself out, spreading his weight. The roof held. He slid down an inch at a time and waited at the bottom for Kate to writhe her way down towards him.

'This time' – he raised his arms to ease her down the last few feet – 'we take no chances. There was talk, was there not, of the Governor paying a visit of inspection to Parramatta? By now he must be here. And wherever his lodging may be, that's where we go – and we don't leave for home until I have a duplicate of that permit from his own hand.'

Governor Bourke's fist slammed down on the table. 'Damn, Harwood, this is a pretty disreputable tale. What have you to say about it?'

Major Harwood stood to attention, not letting his gaze stray towards Kate Bell and Samuel Firbeck. In a clipped, impersonal tone he rapped out: 'Extraordinary, Your Excellency. I'll make inquiries.'

'*You'll* make them? The next inquiry, Harwood, had well be less partial than your last.' The Governor lifted from the top of a sheaf of documents the findings of the court before which Kate had appeared. Irately he waved it at the major. 'There's a damned conspiracy here. Whoever's at fault will be run from this colony. D'you understand?'

'Yes, Excellency.'

'The magistrates are hereby suspended. Your own implication I shall take under personal review. Surgeon-General Hall . . .' Bourke shook his head, at a loss.

'Perhaps a passage to England?' ventured Harwood.

'Best to save a major scandal, I suppose. We're only just recovering from that of my predecessor. Hm, yes, I'll consider that.' The Governor expelled a furious breath, then allowed himself a more leisurely smile as he turned to Samuel. 'Mr Firbeck, I regret the indignities you have suffered. See that your father hears of my deep concern for this mistreatment. I promise you safe conduct to your home.'

'Thank you, sir.'

'As to you, my child' – the Governor indicated that Kate should approach, and reached for his quill – 'I shall grant you a full pardon. Stay with the Firbecks: you need such people to guide you. But you are free of all punishment, and may come and go as you please.'

This time there was no hasty escape. This time Samuel made doubly and then trebly sure that their documents were in order. When they rode away they did so at a formal, confident pace, with their heads held high – though Kate still found it strange that the two troopers accompanying them should be there for their protection rather than their persecution.

The miles fell agreeably away. Kate spoke little. She was still too unaccustomed to the vastness of freedom and fresh air all about her; too dazzled, too unsure of the present and its meaning, let alone of the future which lay beyond the Blue Mountains. From time to time Samuel smiled reassuringly. But it would take many smiles, and many months and a whole new way of life to reassure and heal her.

He sang, inviting her to join in the simple, lilting melody. But her voice refused to harmonize. Perhaps, deep down, she feared it would make a fool of her – bring bad luck and put the clock back yet again.

They passed families on the move, supply wagons, and the usual miscellany of shiftless wanderers along the route. An occasional patrol crossed their path and exchanged salutes.

And at last, where the trail narrowed through the mountains, a familiar figure rode towards them. Samuel shaded his eyes, hardly expecting to see this face so far from their home territory.

'Edward!'

Lieutenant Elliott rode up. The troopers stopped and saluted.

'We were growing worried about you. I was riding back to see what had happened. And what do I find?' He gave Samuel a mock-respectful nod. 'An escort.'

'The Governor's, no less. Edward, this is Kate.'

'Your servant, ma'am. Perhaps I may have the pleasure of taking over escort duty?'

'As far as the border, Edward.' Samuel grinned at Kate. 'We mustn't tempt him across it – he has already acquired enough trouble that way.'

Kate did not understand the two men's easy laughter, but a faint glimmer of a smile broke through.

The troopers were dismissed, glad to turn back from the unfamiliar terrain towards the barracks and taverns and streets where they would be less exposed. Edward Elliott, with a deferential nod to Kate, took charge and set a steady pace uphill, as if to conduct them personally into the very heart of the clouds piled along the ridges.

They rode; rested; rode, camped, slept, and set off again. Kate washed in a stream, pulled her hair back, and held herself more proudly when she returned. But there was still a deep reservoir of disbelief in her – disbelief sparkling in her eyes when, at her approach, Lieutenant Elliott scrambled courteously to his feet.

Samuel began to identify hillocks and plantations and the blazes of other settlers. The ridge ahead was, at last, the one before the village.

'Some of our friends,' he warned Kate, 'are a strange lot. But it's a good place compared with what we've left behind.'

From a distance they could see a number of people in the street. Moll was easily identifiable, waving a bottle and mouthing something from *The Trooper's Rest* across at her husband's store. It was reassuring to find so little altered.

But as they drew closer Samuel noticed an unusual, unnatural hump on the veranda of the inn. Some drunkard, already happily insensible in the middle of the day?

'Here he is!' A couple of men and women turned towards

Lieutenant Elliott accusingly. 'Leaving us . . . talk of protection, and *this* . . .'

The slumped shape was that of an aborigine, thrown casually over a log on the veranda. When Edward Elliott, dismounting, stooped to raise a shoulder of the body from the log, it was messily obvious that the man had been shot – in the back.

CHAPTER TEN

Men and women from the shacks down the street and back lanes of the village began to congregate below the inn veranda, waiting for Elliott's reaction.

He turned to face them. 'Who did this?'

Moll, in proprietorial stance and cradling a bottle to her bosom, cackled. 'What difference does it make? It's one black the less. Who cares?'

'The law cares,' snapped Edward. 'A black man has the same right to our protection as a white man has.'

There was a resentful mutter from the little crowd. Muttering about settlers murdered along the Murray river, shepherds found dead in the bush, sheep stolen or riddled with spears.

'What *about* protecting us, then,' one man jibed, 'from those spears?'

Edward drew himself up. 'I have four soldiers, two constables – and six hundred square miles of land to patrol. I can't be everywhere at once.'

'Get more soldiers.'

'Think we want to be murdered in our beds?'

Moll said something in an undertone and seemed highly delighted by her own sense of humour.

An older man, more serious and less aggressive, shouldered his way to the front. 'They're getting out of hand, there's just no arguing about it. You can *feel* something's gone wrong, there'll be an unholy outbreak soon. We do have to have reinforcements.'

Edward Elliott nodded. 'I'll make application and see what can be done.'

'Before it's too late,' said the man warningly.

Suddenly Samuel espied a grizzled, thoughtful face on the rim of the crowd. Slipping from his horse he beckoned Kate to dismount. She looked warily at the heads of a few women turning towards her, smiling knowingly; then slid from the saddle and fell into step with Samuel.

'This is my father. Father, I've brought Kate to live with us.'

'Thought you were never going to catch up with me.' Jason clasped Kate's hand warmly. 'I was beginning to get a mite worried.'

Samuel laughed. 'Not nearly as worried as we were!'

As they rode out of the village Samuel told the story of their adventures. It occupied most of the journey. Occasionally Kate nodded to underline some point he was making, but added no opinion of her own. She seemed to be mutely opening her senses to each impression of the countryside they passed through; sometimes lulled by it, every now and then starting at some unexpected sound. Perhaps the talk of rebellious blacks worried her. Or perhaps the sheer sounds and feelings of freedom were still so new that they unbalanced her.

'There!' said Jason at last, waving his arm and inviting her to enjoy her first sight of the homestead.

Samuel tried to see it through Kate's eyes. It was difficult. To him each stone and length of timber represented hours of work, and the whole scene was the arduous assembly of all those hours. A stranger could never see or savour it as they, the Firbecks, did.

He wondered how long she would remain a stranger.

They rode down past the barn. Luke came out, dragging on a sweat-stained shirt.

'You took your time.'

He was about to walk away when Samuel said: 'Can you not at least welcome Kate?'

Luke stopped and eyed Kate as he might have eyed a

potential brood mare. When their eyes met he held her gaze until she broke away.

Fuming, Samuel began to bark orders. Shep was commanded to set a fire under the cauldron and provide bath water for the newcomer. Two of Jassy's old dresses, left behind but never thrown away – in this world of uncertainties and shortage you never threw anything away – were taken out, shaken, and left for Kate to make a choice.

When she appeared in the kitchen, bathed, her hair combed back, thin but sleek in the faded cotton dress, Samuel felt again that pang of longing which had twisted through him that early morning by the stream.

Lamely he said: 'Kate, you look . . . much better.'

Luke did not even appear to look round; but he grinned dourly to himself.

In the days which followed, Kate began diffidently to speak: at first only in connection with the work she was taking on, then gradually at greater length. Conversation was an old habit which she had to learn all over again. Samuel derived a happiness he had never known from watching her sway down the slope to the stream, from hearing snatches of sound from her lips adding up to a song, from seeing all the damaged, torn fragments mend at last into a new wholeness.

Only Luke seemed indifferent. But Luke's surliness was a natural hazard she would have to get used to, as they had all got used to it. A phenomenon like drought or wind or thunderstorm: you had to find your own way of coping with it, your own way of settling your own fears.

Luke had always had things on his mind, though they seemed darker and more crushing since Jassy had left. One look, and he had decided Kate was no substitute for Jassy. But then, what substitute would he ever find?

Luke slowed to a trot, coughing against the thin black ash

stirred up by his horse's hoofs. They had to cross a wide patch where a bush fire had raged unchecked until it came to the curve of the river and spent itself along the banks. Luke, impatient, was glad to break free from the charred expanse and up the sheltered hill. The sound of his approach brought Morgan scrambling out of his temporary bark hut, no more than a few strips lashed to a tree.

'Everything all right?'

Morgan tried a cocky salute which failed to come off.

'Out with it, man,' said Luke. 'How many?'

Morgan groped under the lean-to and drew out two feathered spears.

'I've told you' – Luke leaned menacingly down – 'if blacks cross the river, you're to shoot 'em.'

'But I didn't even see them. Didn't see nothin'.'

'Better do something to improve your eyesight, then. Because you'll pay for losses out of your rations.'

Morgan glowered. 'They'll be goin' to feed black bellies, is it, mister?'

'They'll feed who I choose.'

'Talkin' of shootin' 'em one minute, then playin' around with 'em the next – don't make no sense. Don't you see, it's like the folk in the village say, it's – '

Luke edged his horse closer. He hit Morgan across the side of the head and left him where he lay, riding off towards the farther loop of the river and the dark trees and the warm, welcoming night beyond.

The chief waited in the firelight. Luke dropped a sack of provisions on the hard, trampled ground by the fire. And dropped a sheep carcass from his crupper.

'Bacca?' said the chief hopefully.

Luke took a twist from his pocket and held it out, not letting go. 'Who's killing my sheep?'

'No sheep.'

'*Master*.'

'No sheep, master.' The chief continued to stare at the twist of tobacco.

'You lying bastard. Somebody's killing my sheep, and not because you need the meat. Just for the sake of killing. Who is it?'

The girl stood on the other side of the fire. He beckoned her closer. As her haunches swung in the smoky glow he felt the burning start within him. And saw a burning of something as fierce in other eyes: smouldering hatred in the face of a young aborigine who had been standing beside the girl. Quite capable of killing sheep just in a rage of jealousy. For all the good that would do him.

The girl stood meekly by his booted heel. Luke took out a necklace of crudely hammered little horseshoes and dropped it neatly, casually over her sleek brown neck. Her fingers were quick to touch it, and her tongue dabbed a promise between her gleaming teeth.

Luke dismounted and stood for a moment over the chief. 'I've told you more than once. Keep your side of the river and out of trouble, and I'll see you get supplies. Cross it – you're dead men. Don't you understand a bargain?'

'Understand . . . master.'

At last the twist of tobacco fell beside him.

Luke took the girl's hand and led her past the old man and past the younger. 'If it's you, Yabba, killing my stock, I'll slit your black throat.' The words would convey nothing, but the tone of voice left as little doubt about his meaning as Yabba's eyes left of his own feelings.

Nor did the girl – whose name he did not even know – grasp any of his words; but understood all he needed her to understand. Her sly fingers, her mouth, her sweat and her frenzy were all that mattered. He liked to carry the smell of her away with him on his body. No need for anything more complicated. Yet every now and then he would find himself talking meaninglessly to her as if to establish some other bond. He wanted no bond – yet was somehow not content with unvarying silence. Tonight, sprawled on a blanket under the rock, he called her a cannibal and a whore, and laughed. And she laughed uncomprehendingly. 'Stone Age strumpet,' he reviled her. They met, he thought helplessly, across a million years. He cursed her; coaxed her. And she stroked her necklace, letting it rise and fall against her hot, damp flesh.

Yabba could talk to her. But perhaps he would not want to, after this. Yabba proved himself a great lover by killing sheep, showing himself unafraid of the white man's thunder-stick. But in the end, despite tribal customs and choices, he might not want to be a lover. Or she might no longer want him.

One day, perhaps, there would be a spear in Luke Firbeck's own back?

He reached for the girl again. With his nameless black velvet he was comfortable in the velvet night. In the morning he would be Luke Firbeck, master of all he surveyed, and afraid of no man.

He rode away unscathed, with no more than a 'Watch that fire – we want no bush blazes along *my* boundaries'. This tribe would not lay a finger on him: the chief valued his tobacco and grog too highly. If ever things got bad enough to warrant action against Yabba or any other sheep-slayer, the chief was the one to take that action.

When he reached the homestead Luke found he had cause to debate whether that time had not, perhaps, come. Three dead sheep lay with their stupid, dead faces staring vacantly up the slope above the barn. Shep, trembling, was talking and waving his hands agitatedly at Jason.

'Why?' Jason demanded as Luke rode into earshot. 'There's no rhyme or reason. It's not as if they were taking the meat.'

'Revenge, mister,' quavered Shep.

'If they want revenge,' said Luke, joining them, 'they shall have it. Mine.'

Shep gave him a half scared, half accusing look, but did not dare to pass on any hints or speculations to Jason.

Before Luke could make any angry inquiries, there was the sound of hoofs down the trail from the village. A corporal and two troopers rode in past the Firbeck stock pens. Luke could not recall having seen any of the men before: they did not appear to belong to Edward Elliott's garrison. He set himself beside his father and waited to find what trouble portended.

'Corporal Bailey, gents, of the Seventeenth. Sent as reinforcements to Lieutenant Elliott's command. Heard the blacks settling in a bit too close for comfort, right?'

'You've come a long way, Corporal,' said Jason affably. 'Some ale?'

'Why, in this God-forsaken place I never thought to hear words like that.' The corporal tried an endearing smile. The creases of his face were not practised in such a formation. 'A gentleman's greeting, sir!'

'Your horses can graze over there.' Jason cleared his throat, seizing a rare opportunity to play the expansive landowner. 'Allow me to introduce myself. I am Jason Firbeck, and you are at the moment on Firbeck property. My property.'

The corporal froze. 'Jason Firbeck?'

'You've heard the name? From Lieutenant Elliott, possibly – my son-in-law.'

'Elliott,' said Corporal Bailey softly. 'Your son-in-law, eh? No, not from him. Not from him it wasn't.'

Jason took the corporal and his two men round the side of the house. Luke watched them go. For himself, he had been strongly tempted to send the patrol briskly on their way. A poor sort of protection men of that calibre would offer, if protection were needed! They were more of a menace than an ally – edging a way in from the Nineteen Counties, prying in territories which had managed without military protection or interference during the difficult times and could well manage without it now. But once his father played the magnanimous host there was no stopping him.

Luke stabled his horse and went back to work in the barn, where he had been strengthening the loft and fashioning a new hoist for the end of the gable. From the small forge near the stream he heard Samuel tapping away at a pulley-wheel and hooks for the hoist.

Out of nowhere came a wild scream. Luke stooped below a rafter, reached the gable opening, and swung the flap to one side.

Below he saw Kate, thunderstruck, motionless on the path from the river. She bore a tub of washing on her shoulder, and seemed to have been petrified where she stood.

In the back doorway of the house stood Corporal Bailey with a mug of ale. He was grinning uncontrollably as he stepped out into the sunlight.

'Well, well. If it isn't little Kate.'

'No.' From where Luke was, high above, it sounded no more than a whisper.

'Oh, but yes. Does seem we're fated, my beauty, you and I.'

She shrieked again. 'Get him away!' And as she dropped the load of washing, Bailey roared his delight.

Samuel came out of the forge and began to run across the grass. Luke, curious, leaned farther out. Quite a scene they were performing for his benefit.

Samuel reached the corporal and stared, incredulous, into his face. 'You . . . !' Then he held up his fist and slowly clenched it. 'Get off this land.'

'Now, see here – '

'Off this land. And if you open your filthy mouth or ever

attempt to say one word to that lady, I'll shut it for you.'

Ale slopped out of the mug as the corporal backed away. Jason appeared, outraged, on the step.

'Samuel, what right have you to address . . .'

Kate was running, weaving a wild path away from the house, under the barn and away down the slope. One of the troopers darted from behind his corporal and sprinted to cut her off. Panting, she was caught in his embrace.

'Hold hard, little 'un. No one's going to hurt you.'

However kindly his intention, he held her too tightly and too long. Her claws raked three crimson gashes down his cheek to his jaw. He let her go, and she was off again. Then Samuel began to run, calling after her, trying to keep his voice steady as he stumbled and raced on.

They were out of Luke's line of vision now. But by the time he got down from the loft, Samuel was leading the girl back – leading her well away from Corporal Bailey, into the house by the veranda.

That evening Luke lounged in the kitchen doorway, abstractedly watching the flicker of a small fire near the soldiers' two tents. A few lines of a bawdy song drifted towards him, then a burst of laughter. He turned back into the kitchen.

Kate leaned over the fire. All her buoyancy had gone. Each time anyone spoke to her she flinched. A score of times in as many minutes she glanced at the door, waiting for Bailey to reappear.

Samuel said: 'That swine of a corporal has got to take himself off. We don't want him here.'

Luke leaned against the door jamb, summing them up. Samuel was already becoming too fond of the girl. Poor, susceptible Samuel! He had nearly made a fool of himself over that slut Nora, the Shipton woman, so long ago. And now he was ripe for another misadventure – with a hell-cat straight out of the most appalling training-ground for vice and depravity in New South Wales. They needed a woman in the household, but did it have to be one such? Standing by the fire where Jassy had stood, washing and cooking and mending as Jassy had done. But she must not presume to insinuate herself into their lives in the hope of becoming all that Jassy had once been. She was here on sufferance. It would do her no great harm to be cowed, as she was now.

Jason shifted uneasily. 'After what you have told us about that man, I'm less happy that he should be on our land. Perhaps if we reported to Edward – '

'I think Bailey should stay.' Luke came out with it, and saw Kate crouch almost double over a cooking pot.

'The man means nothing but ill,' said Samuel. 'I fear for our safety – above all for Kate's.'

'Pray his duties soon take him elsewhere,' said his father.

Luke ground out a laugh. 'Everyone in the region was begging for protection. Now we have it. You wanted law: there it is, outside – fine upstanding guardians of your cherished English justice.'

'They must go.'

Luke had thought so in the moment of their arrival. His mistrust of uniforms and all they stood for had not abated. But now he saw another side; and was drily amused.

'Cross that corporal, and he'll be away to the authorities with just the complaint some of them are waiting to hear. Squatters stir up trouble with the aborigines, and then reject the help of the law. They're rebels, bad citizens. How long d'you think it would be before that was turned into an excuse to clear us off our land?'

'Our rights are being recognized,' said Jason. 'Commissioners are being appointed. The land will be ours. No more talk of driving us off.'

'The land will be ours for just as long as we can hold it. Who do you think their commissioners will be? Honest

Christian men dealing fairly with every hard-working man they encounter? Father, it's not your time, not your world. The reality is out there – the power's out there – with your corporal friend.'

Samuel flared up. 'I'll not have that scum called friend of anyone in this – '

'He stays,' said Luke, 'for as long as he can contrive it. He and his men cost us nothing but food and ale. And their faces may frighten the sheep killers off, even if their uniforms don't.'

Whatever might have happened in the past, it became clear to Luke during the next few days that Bailey had a grudge to pay off. He was not going to attack Samuel, whatever might have passed between them: he knew his orders and his limitations too well for that. But Kate was still, so far as he was concerned, fair prey. He prowled around her, tormenting her without a word in the presence of others. And when others were not there? Luke could guess. He recognized lust when he saw it, and recognized the deep desire for revenge. Bailey was a cunning rat: if Jason or Samuel appeared, his words became innocent and respectful. If Luke crossed his and Kate's path, there was no more than an understanding silence. Bailey knew pretty well where Luke stood, but also knew well enough not to presume too openly on it.

And the ostensible reason for the patrol's operations in the district could not be sneered at. Flagrant attacks on the sheep had diminished. The threat of the redcoats was useful – in more ways than one.

He used it one morning as he left the dark arms and loins of the girl beyond the river – a girl so much simpler and so much less trouble than the white wild cat Samuel had brought into their midst.

'Where's Yabba?'

For once there had been no lowering, malevolent eyes

watching him as he led the girl away, or as he brought her back to the ashes of the camp fire in the morning.

Still muzzy, giggling slightly from last night's grog, the chief shook his head.

'I have three soldiers who want to drive you away,' Luke threatened. 'I think you've seen them, yes? A word from me, they'll have you on the move. So everything goes as I say. Right? If Yabba starts up killing my sheep again, I might just tell the soldiers to come. They will probably kill you.'

The chief tipped up the empty mug and sadly watched three tiny drops fall to the dry earth.

'Tell your brothers,' said Luke, 'no more sheep. No more killing. Yabba starts it again, and – well, I think perhaps you must act. Quickly. Understand?'

He left the chief to think about it, and rode back to the homestead.

Even from a distance he knew something was badly wrong. Morgan, neglecting a straying confusion of sheep, was bending fearfully over something on the hillside. Shep stood some way off, not venturing a step nearer. If they had let something go so wrong that they were frightened now, it was nothing compared with what they would feel when Luke had his say.

He spurred on towards them.

Morgan stood back. 'Oh, mister, you done it now.'

Sprawled on the slope above the homestead, a splash of red jacket in the dark green and brown of the landscape, was the body of Corporal Bailey. He might have been in a drunken stupor. But he was not. A spear had been driven deep into his chest, standing up so erect that it appeared almost to have impaled him to the ground.

They heard in the village. Morgan rode in with the news, and added it to the tales already seething in *The Trooper's*

Rest. A soldier stricken down? – this was the worst of the lot. A man and woman carved to pieces on a lonely plot fifty miles away, a woman raped on a small-holding just this side of the hills . . . they were stories from a distance, horrible enough but not yet too close. But a corporal from their own barracks, a man sent out to stop just this kind of thing . . . It showed, didn't it, that the explosion was near? The whole borderland was aflame, the aborigines on the edge of Firbeck territory were only an outpost: there would soon be an entire murderous army closing in for the ghastly slaughter.

'Corporal Bailey,' said Moll in reverent memory. She knew a good customer when she saw one, and she had seen this one more than once. 'Shows you, though – a musket's not much good, not when they've made up their minds.'

'Not one musket, no. A hundred, though . . .'

Lieutenant Edward Elliott felt the heat of panic scorching through the village. His attempts to beat down the flames were unavailing. Nobody was willing to wait any longer. Wait – for reinforcements, for a court of inquiry? They had had their reinforcements and they knew the answer to any inquiry: one of their so-called defenders had been murdered, out there.

When Elliott returned to barracks he sent an urgent messenger to Parramatta. And, as unobtrusively as possible, he sent his wife and her friend Anna along with the military despatch. He was not unobtrusive enough. If the garrison commander wanted his womenfolk out of the way, so did the settlers. Better still, remove the threat to those women-folk – the threat to all of them.

'You know what they do to you?' Moll, jug in hand, was in her element. For the first time the women of the village, scared to be alone, crowded into the tap-room along with their men. 'You think blacks'd be satisfied the way your own sort are? They've got devil's ways in 'em.'

'But what do we do if . . . when . . . ?'

'Best get your men to declare on that, hadn't you? Men!' cried Moll with superb disdain. 'Maybe Rosie and me could pick out the good 'uns among you. But you'd best give 'em a nudge yourselves.'

'That lieutenant's a black-lover, that's what.' A farrier groped for his tankard and pouted out his pigeon chest for his wife's benefit. 'Wouldn't catch me lettin' 'em murder one o' me own men and turnin' me back.'

The decision was not long in coming. If it had taken any longer they might all have grown too soporific to make any decision whatsoever. But with fire in their veins and bellies the men found muskets and axes, and torches and courage – and found the way along the river that made a short cut to the edge of the Firbeck settlement: the edge where the cunning forerunners of the black invasion had made themselves at home.

From the veranda of the Firbeck homestead Samuel heard the first shots, and the shouting, and more shots and sharply slashed screams, wailing back from the hillside.

'For mercy's sake' – Jason peered unavailingly into the night – 'what's happening out there?'

A curl of flame and smoke stained the purity of the starlit sky.

'The blacks,' said Samuel, his head cocked. 'Someone's at them.'

'Get the guns.' Luke was already dashing for the stables. 'I'll saddle the horses.'

Samuel caught a blur of his father's anguish, Kate's fear – and a fleeting memory of Corporal Bailey's twisted, hateful face. One killing had proved the last straw. The death of one evil man whose loss was mourned by nobody could, ironically, ignite a devastating fire.

Father and two sons, wordlessly united for the first time

in many a hard month, rode towards the uproar. It did not abate. The curses became rowdier as they galloped the last mile; the screams more heart-rending.

They stormed at last into the clearing.

A ragged volley of muskets smashed across the opening from their left. Already a tangle of bodies had been destroyed along the rim of the camp fire, and there was the stench of flesh from two men and a woman who had been tossed half-alive on to the flames. One native still brandished a spear, peering half-blind into the insanely cavorting shadows to pick out just one target, just one enemy before he surrendered his own life.

A woman howled among the trees.

'Got 'er,' shouted a jubilant, drunken man's voice. There was another shriek, and silence.

Silence lasted only a second. Branches crashed and splintered. Three figures fought madly near a primitive hut. Samuel saw Luke's face in the firelight, distorted by trailers of smoke. It was stretched in an impossible agony such as he had never thought his brother capable of. Luke was dragging his horse in and out of the dead, the dying, the savagely fighting.

'Finish 'em off.' The exultant shout rang through the leaves and branches.

A child ran into the clearing, eyes stark and bright. Before Samuel could sweep him out of harm's way, three men were upon him.

'Look, 'e's only a nipper, shall we – '

'Grow up to spear a white fella soon enough.'

A knife rose and fell. The tiny body was swung, streaming blood, towards the sputtering funeral pyre.

Luke swung up his carbine. Samuel ranged himself alongside.

'Hold it. All of you. Not a move.'

Some men chuckled and whined away into the shadows.

A couple more emerged and blinked, bewildered as to why anybody should be calling a halt now.

Luke left Samuel by the charnel fireside and edged his horse towards the bushes. Abruptly he stopped. Samuel risked a glance sideways. He saw his brother stoop over a shape sprawled, draped over a tree. And heard him retch and moan something indescribable, and slide whimpering from his horse.

A black girl had been flung across the jagged stump of a tree and cut open at the stomach and neck. Blood ran darker than darkness over her limp legs and down the stump and into the earth, like a dribbling stain of tobacco spittle. Luke reached out and appeared to touch the gash in the throat, just once. When he came reeling back into the light, a stained necklace of glinting, bloody drops hung from his little finger.

'Morgan locked up. It ain't right.' Shep crouched malignantly in the doorway. 'Him an' the rest of 'em, locked up and liable to be tried and hanged and Gawd knows what else – for what? For protecting themselves as best they knew how, for defending themselves instead of mixing . . . *mixing*, that's what . . .'

'Get out,' said Jason sternly, 'and about your work.'

'Aye. Oh, aye.' Shep shuffled off, as near to mutiny as they had ever seen him.

When he had gone, Samuel said: 'What I gathered from Shepherd this morning is little short of incredible.' He challenged Luke across the table. 'I hope you will tell me it is not true.'

Jason, haggard and dazed, dared not look up at his two sons. The Bible was on the table before him. He opened it at random in search of solace. There was silence.

'So it is true,' said Samuel. 'Your appetites – your deceits

– have brought about the slaughter of innocent people. Father, do you not see?'

Jason turned the pages more feverishly.

'Your son,' said Samuel inexorably, 'has consorted with a female black. To avenge this, the tribe killed a drunken redcoat with a spear which more properly belonged in *him*.' He stared at Luke across a great distance. 'You're not my brother. You have gone so far from what we once – '

'Twelve thousand miles,' said Luke. 'The same as you. To a new beginning.'

Kate appeared in the doorway behind him, her hands twisting in the folds of her apron.

'But not to forget what we were,' said Samuel.

'To forget everything. Otherwise there could be no new beginning.' Aware of Kate behind him, Luke swung around. 'What was there worth remembering? Ask this girl what England meant. Nothing but shame – the scars, the indignities, rape, the lash. Here we carve our own world out of our own stone age. And to start, you have to forget old hypocrisies. When things go wrong, you don't look back – you keep going ahead.'

Jason said: 'You will leave my house.'

'Carrying the blame for all your failings? And for every weakling, every village drunkard wanting to play the warrior just once in his wretched life, every – '

'I killed Corporal Bailey,' said Kate.

Jason stared at her pallid drawn face. Luke began to laugh unsteadily, a laugh on the verge of breakdown.

Kate stepped into the room like one in a trance. She said: 'It had become . . . too much for me to bear. I felt alone. You did not see – did not *feel* the venom that was in him. He followed me, he would not let me be, he told me he would take me away and that you would not be interested in stopping him – there were plenty more where I came from – and I didn't believe him but I *did* believe him. Then he tried to . . . I had no strength left, I could manage no longer, he was at the door of my room and then with me at the door of the barn, and he was trying . . .' Breath scraped up from her throat. 'I saw the spears you had collected in the barn. They were all I had. I stopped him – it was all I had left to do.'

Into the tremulous silence, Luke said: 'What do you do now, you fine Christian gentlemen? Throw her to the lions? Send her back where she came from – for other Baileys?'

There was the clatter of hoofs and wheels outside the house. Jason glanced out of the window, then was on his feet. Jassy was getting down from a gig. When she came into the room her father held out his arms, and she ran into them.

Luke watched with a set face as Lieutenant Edward Elliott followed her from the gig.

'Welcome, my boy,' said Jason over Jassy's shoulder.

Edward gave him a military rather than a filial nod.

'I have come to ask for your co-operation.'

'Anything we can do. Anything at all.' Jason dragged chairs into a sociable group. Luke stood back with his arms folded.

Edward said: 'The predicament is a shameful one. I know my duty – but the spirit of the community is against me. Clearly the massacre should not go unpunished – '

'I trust it will not,' said Jason. 'We have preferred the necessary charges, and as eye-witnesses we shall not flinch when the matter is brought to court.'

Jassy slid away from him and close to her husband. Edward went on: 'The village will not stand for their men-folk being locked away. My own men are close to mutiny. One appreciates their feelings. They do not want the prosecution to proceed.'

'But a great wrong has been done. The massacre – '

'Is just one among many wrongs,' said Luke icily.

'There is nothing we can do to turn back the tide of justice. Nor should there be.'

'You could decline to give evidence,' said Edward. 'So that I can withdraw the charges. Truly, I believe we would do best to forget all that has happened.'

'And let drunken murderers go free?'

Edward swallowed, lowering his head. 'Yes.'

'But every principle we stand for . . .' Jason looked from one of his sons to the other, begging their support. 'You'd have us all – '

'Hypocrites,' said Luke.

'I can't do it.'

'Please, father,' Jassy ventured unhappily.

He consulted Samuel. 'Must I?'

They waited. At last Samuel said: 'I think so. I think that is how it must be. There are so many things which . . . shouldn't be said.'

'So the innocent must die, unsung?'

'That the bad may live, father,' said Luke, 'like kings.'

CHAPTER ELEVEN

The woolshed was piled high with bales. The dealer gestured along floor and shelving, shaking his head over the sample Luke had tugged from the dray.

'It's been a good year. Plenty about – see for yourself. Doesn't help the price, of course.'

'No, of course,' said Luke without a flicker of a smile.

'Things being as they are,' said Dogget, 'I could just about go to twenty pence a pound.'

Luke reached for the sample. 'I'll take it through to Sydney.'

'Hold hard, hold hard.' Dogget fingered the wool expertly. 'Not bad quality. Twenty-three.'

'No.'

'You won't do better.'

'Thirty-five,' said Luke, 'or I'll be on my way.'

'Twenty-six.'

They played the game with cool mutual appreciation. When Luke had agreed to fill his wagon for the return journey with supplies from Dogget's adjoining store, a price adjustment was found possible. They jockeyed for further advantage, and finally settled on thirty pence a pound.

Stocking up, Luke's attention was caught by a music-box among the racks of pots, pans, bedding and trinkets. While Dogget totted up a bill, he lifted the lid and released a tinkling thread of tune, as sweet as a rippling brook. Two men farther along the counter, waiting to be served, glanced sidelong at him and grinned.

'Forty-nine shillings, that,' said Dogget without looking up from his calculations.

'Add it on.'

'For the wife?'

'Sister.'

There was a snicker from one of the men beside him. 'One and the same thing where some of 'em come from.'

Luke closed the box, braced himself, and swung both closed fists into the lout's face so that he went spinning back into the middle of the sacks, boxes and barrels.

He was glad to be on his homeward way, out in the good clean air away from township or village, driving his bullocks on over the mountains and the western plain into the great panorama of earth and sky. The wind was uncomfortably dry, though. Ominously large stretches of ground were burnt and blackened, ragged with tree butts.

The music-box was safely packed in a nest of straw, within a wooden box. From time to time he stopped to camp, or to make a meal of damper and mutton, he opened it and let the plaintive little tune drift away through the trees.

He looked forward to seeing Jassy's face when he set it before her and she raised the lid.

There was a far from musical sound resonating through the village when he plodded eventually down the dry, dusty street. In the light of early morning Edward Elliott and a trooper were leaving the barracks at the rear of a convict file. Moll was up and about, making *The Trooper's Rest* anything but restful. She had her fingers locked in the neck-band of a wizened little man with a nose like a weasel's, and her stentorian soprano ensured that nobody should sleep any longer.

'Won't, is it?' She snatched up a broom from the veranda and belaboured the cowering wretch. 'Won't? We'll see who won't and who will.'

At a word from Elliott, the trooper detached himself from the work party and crossed the street.

'What's up?'

'He won't pay.'

'I paid 'er, honest,' whined the man.

'Not the extra, you didn't.'

'Extra?' queried the trooper dubiously.

Luke swung down from the dray and began to slacken a tarpaulin fastening. Moll yelled across at him. 'This one here doesn't know what *extras* are!'

Luke grinned and waved. Rosie came to the door and leaned there, eyeing him without much optimism. Seeing her, the trooper caught the meaning. 'Oh, extras! But . . . *him*?'

'She was as keen for it as I was.' The man fell to his knees, shielding his head against the flailing broom.

Edward Elliott joined them. 'Leave him alone.'

'I'll leave him alone when you take him off my hands. Go on – take him and lock him up till he pays what he owes.'

'Extras are – um – outside our jurisdiction.' The lieutenant stood above the cowering man. 'What's your name?'

'Nipper. Nipper Clarke.'

'Had a bit of trouble with you before, haven't we?'

'Look, mister . . . sir . . . all I want is to be on me way, don't mean no harm, it ain't right . . .'

'Where are you heading?'

'West.'

Edward looked round. 'Luke, you in need of anyone? Or willing to take him off my territory, anyway?'

'He can ride with me. Give me a hand along the way.' He lifted the small box from beneath the tarpaulin. 'I'll be on my way soon. Just call in and see Jass.'

His brother-in-law pursed his lips; then turned back to the work party. Luke went on up the street to the barracks, and round to the Elliotts' quarters in the shade of a plantation at the back.

Jassy answered the door to him in a nightdress with a

shawl drawn over her shoulders. Surprise at this early morning caller came slowly: she was still drowsily warm from her bed, slow and dreamy and glowing.

'Luke, how lovely. I wasn't expecting you.'

She held the door open and he walked in, closing it behind him and walking on through a tiny room until he found himself within a few paces in her bedroom. He placed the music-box in the middle of the rumpled counterpane.

Jassy, curious, lifted the lid.

'Oh, Luke.' The first clear little notes seemed to strike tears from her eyes.

He caught her arm. She said, 'How lovely, oh it's so pretty', and moved away from him.

'What is it?' he demanded. 'What's wrong?'

She could only shake her head.

'Tell me. Is it Edward? Is he – '

'Luke, please. It's nothing. Don't.'

'It won't do, will it?' He barred her way, caught her by the shoulders. The tune rose and fell despairingly. 'I told you it was wrong.'

'There's nothing wrong. Truly. I think I'm a disappointment, I think Edward . . . but no, I'm not awake properly, I don't know what I'm . . . Luke, it's just that I wasn't ready for you. Wasn't expecting to see you. Luke, please – I'm all right.'

'I love you, Jass.' When she tried to wrench free he held her facing him. The warm night smell was still on her. Her lower lip was slack and trembling. 'Why don't we go away, right away from all this? From Edward, from father, this whole trap – out where it's clean. You and I belong to each other.'

'No.'

'Why don't you face it?' He shook her gently. 'You know it's true.'

She touched his face with questioning fingers, and he

could hold back no longer. He kissed her, and kissed her savagely again, and buried his lips in the softness of her throat.

The door clicked open.

Jassy tried to pull away. Her husband crossed the room, speechless. The music-box started its melody all over again, abruptly cut off as Edward slammed the lid down. He picked up the box and held it out to Luke.

'Out,' His voice was numb with shock. 'And stay out.'

The dray rumbled along the track away from the village. Walking beside the bullocks, Luke cracked his whip repeatedly against their hides. Their pace did not alter.

Nipper Clarke sat perkily on the seat. When Luke at last got tired of trudging through the dust and clambered up beside him, he said matily: 'Nice day.' And then: 'Much work about? Wouldn't want a man yourself, maybe?'

When he realized he would get no response, he shrugged, whistled tunelessly to himself for a while, and made no further comment until they approached a swollen ford.

'Level's rising a bit – that's a freak for you, eh?'

Luke scowled. The land and woodlands were as dry as tinder, yet the water swirled thick and brown and deep. It was a mad country. You could get a flood, suffer your animals and half your belongings washed away, right in the middle of a drought.

They plunged into the ford, lurching perilously, and nearly came to grief halfway across when one wheel went heavily down into a pot-hole. The bullocks strained and scrabbled free. But two miles farther on there was a long squawk of tortured wood, a crack, and the axle broke.

When the wagon had ceased tilting, the two men got down gingerly.

'Now what do we do?' asked Nipper.

'Get it unloaded.'

The little man contemplated the piles of sacks and boxes. The cockiness fled from his face. He began to frame a protest.

'Work or walk,' said Luke. 'It's up to you.'

He began to unfasten the lashings, and swung the nearest sack on to his back. When he had lowered it to a clear patch of ground ten yards away, he jerked a thumb to indicate that Nipper should take over and stack everything neatly, in the right order. Hefting an axe, he went into the trees in search of a new axle.

It would at best be makeshift, unseasoned and liable to twist. But it would get them home. He found a reasonable trunk and began to hack it down.

Just as it fell and he was about to start lopping the branches, he heard a faint, reminiscent sound. It might have been a breath of melancholy wind, or water trickling over near-by stones.

Then he recognized it. It was the sound of the music-box.

Luke paced slowly and deliberately back to the clearing. The music grew louder. Through a gap in the trees he saw Nipper Clarke with a rum bottle to his lips and a length of new curtain material draped over his shoulders, waltzing over the grass and the stones of the track. In his free arm he cradled the music-box. The tune tinkled incessantly as Luke walked to the dray and slid the whip from its slot by the driving seat.

Nipper turned and saw him. The waltz came to an end in the middle of a bar.

Luke said: 'Put it down.'

Nipper carefully set the music-box on the ground.

'Step away.'

Nipper shuffled to one side. 'Now look, mister . . .' He clutched the rum bottle and lifted one arm defensively.

The whip came up. Lashed out. Nipper yelled. He tried to stumble away, but the whip followed and tore into him.

The bottle fell and broke. The music rippled steadily on, broken by an unrhythmic belch of screams and pleas and, at last, sobs dying away under the prim steadiness of the melody.

The tune began its stately measure again in the lee of the barn. Luke nodded Kate towards it and said: 'A present for you.'

'For me?' A muscle moved in her forearm. Despite herself, her legs began gently to dance.

'I hope you like it,' he said.

She looked at him, pirouetted, and stopped; happy beyond imagining, yet scared of its happening so swiftly, out of nowhere.

Luke went back into the house and tossed his hat and whip on the table.

Jason said: 'You can't be serious – about what you said, a few minutes ago, when you arrived?'

'You reckon not?' Luke gazed through the window at the low hills and at something far beyond which only he could see.

'But we've been here for years now. How many years has it taken us to build this up?' Jason groped through the past. 'And we're just beginning to make it look like home. Like a real home. Close the curtains, and sometimes I feel we could be back in England.'

'But we're not.'

'Move on – now, after so much? There are families in the Dales haven't moved for a hundred years. More. Remember the Ogilvies? Heavens, they were there from Cromwell's time.'

'Out there,' said Luke, 'is a million acres. Never an axe, never the tread of a boot.'

'You led us out here. We could have shared a very comfortable grant of land. But we followed you, and we've built it up, and at last we've got something to be proud of. And you want us to move on again?'

'After all we've done.' Samuel added his protest.

'All we've done,' said Luke. 'Just so. We've built a prison. Curtains, paddocks, father's stables, cosy little chairs and . . .' He tossed his head back, as if fighting off unwanted memories crowding in from every corner of the room. 'It's time to put it behind us. We didn't come all this way just to stagnate. We didn't leave drabness behind simply in order to create another drabness out of *this* world.'

'What's wrong with permanence?' Jason demanded. 'What's wrong with being solid and settled and God-fearing and content? What's wrong with *you*, boy?'

Samuel, awkwardly edging out of the conflict, took Luke's whip to move it from the table. He ran his fingers along it, and inspected them.

'You've been flogging those beasts again.' He held out reddened fingertips towards his father. 'One of these days he'll kill something.'

The corpse lay on a board, set across two trestles in the barracks. It was a small, pitiful corpse. Lieutenant Edward Elliott stood at one side, waiting for Luke Firbeck to answer him.

Luke studied the puffy, crinkled, dead face.

'Yes,' he said.

'This is the man who left the village with you that day?'

'Don't be so bloody pompous. You know he was. It was you who foisted him off on me.'

'That's all you have to say?'

'What more do you want me to say?'

The lieutenant turned the body slightly to show the ends of scars which had crept over the left shoulder, encrusted with blood which had then been smeared and softened by water.

'Did you flog him?'

'Yes.'

'Why?'

'He tried to rob me.'

'Would you say that could have caused his death?'

'By drowning?' said Luke caustically.

'You think he was drowned?'

'Don't you? I understood he was found – '

'Because he was found in a creek,' said Edward, 'that doesn't mean he died in the creek. Killers have been known to disguise their crimes.'

Luke did not deign to reply.

'There'll be a doctor,' said Edward, 'as soon as we can get him here. He'll tell us if Nipper Clarke drowned – or died some other way. In the meantime, I think you'd better stay here, where we can get at you.'

Luke grabbed Edward's lapel. 'What the hell are you trying to do?' The stony stare he received told him all there was to tell. 'So that's it. I should have guessed you'd come for me one of these days.'

Edward shook his hand away. He called, and a trooper clicked his heels in the doorway.

'Lock him up.'

He had been in the cell block for less than an hour when he had his first visitor. It was Jassy, white and tense. Whatever had passed between her and her husband had left her badly shaken. She tried to put an arm through the bars to touch Luke, but he paced away to the back of his cell – a caged animal unwilling to be soothed, but not yet desperate enough to claw and bite back.

Jassy brought food in that day and the next. And the third time she brought Samuel with her, his eyes reddened and scorched by dust from the journey. The two of them leaned their foreheads against the bars.

Samuel said: 'Luke, you've got to speak. Not to anyone

else, but to me. Tell me you didn't kill that man, so that I may set father's mind at rest.'

'He'll believe you?' said Luke indifferently.

'If you speak the truth, I shall know and believe you, and father will believe.'

'Does it matter?'

'Doesn't it matter, then?' When Luke made no reply, Samuel looked at his sister. 'Surely Edward will not press these charges? We have stood by him in the past, when he has needed us. Surely now . . .'

'One of the family and all that,' said Luke.

'Well?' Samuel challenged Jassy. 'Will he?'

Her agonized face told him nothing for his comfort. And beyond her, their caged brother sneered back at them with the naked scorn of a man who had seen the ultimate ludicrousness of it all – the fate which he had always expected to turn treacherously on him, and which had now done so.

Jassy wept. 'Luke, you must tell *me*. That man . . . did you . . . ?'

He looked bleakly at her, then away at the wall.

Jason sat by the fire, trying to read. Kate was clearing the table. The room seemed twice its usual size, filled with unnatural echoes. One expected a footfall at the door and a clash of voices which did not come.

Kate hesitated at Jason's elbow.

'Will there be any news?'

'Sooner or later there will have to be some. I fear it will be only to the bad.' He creaked back in his chair. 'Only the worst.'

'He couldn't have done it,' she said.

'He could all too well have done it.'

'No. He's a hard man, your Luke. But I do not believe that of him.'

'Be about your business.' Jason scraped his chair fretfully

round. 'You can't know him as we do, girl. His character . . . oh, God, he's my own son but I have to say I could have wished it . . . a little different.'

Her eyes were hot with an emotion strange to Jason. Strange, perhaps, to herself also. She said: 'He's afraid.'

'As well he might be.'

'I mean that when he's here, in this place, he's afraid. All the time.'

'He has shown precious little sign of it. Now be about your work,' he ordered again.

'Because no one helps him, no one tries to understand.'

'You know nothing about it.'

'He's a boy,' she cried, 'doing the job of a man. You expected too much of him. I saw it, I *know*, I know it was too much for anybody. Did he ever let you down? Leave you to fend for yourselves, leave you to grapple with anything he hadn't already made easy for you?'

Jason opened the Bible with heavy deliberation and bent over it to show that he meant his dismissal. But after she had left the room he found it impossible to read.

Jason sat a long time, hearing the sounds of Kate's activity in the scullery and at the back of the house. She was good at her work. He had to grant her that, and was glad to do so. There was no task she would not turn her hand to, and her sheer gratitude at being here made her in many ways an even more devoted helper than Jassy had been. Samuel had chosen well. So long as Samuel was not so foolish as to fall in love with the wench, all would be well for all of them.

For Luke . . . ?

He was staring into the unknown when a jumble of sounds cut across what Kate was doing. There was a shout, followed by a scurry of feet, and then hoofs and more shouting, and the slam of a door.

'Master! Master!'

When he hurried out of the back door it was to find the sky beyond the ridge glowing with a light they had never seen before, a light which soared and pulsed and cast an eerie dawn across the treetops.

'Fire, master – fire!' Morgan slid to a halt before him, breathless. 'And it's blowing this way.'

'Fire?'

The bright throbbing beat up behind the hill, and now there was the tang of bitter smoke on the air. It was close: too close. And his two able-bodied sons were far away: too far.

CHAPTER TWELVE

Jassy stopped each time she passed the window, to look vainly out at a patch of the barrack square and one corner of the cell block. Edward watched her and several times began a protest, but checked himself. She would have been glad if he had spoken; was trying to goad him into complaining, so that she could turn on him and spill out all her anger.

She was the first to give way. Carrying a heavy earthenware pot from the kitchen, she could bear it no longer. Deliberately she hurled it to the floor at his feet. There was a satisfying crash.

'He has not been found guilty,' she cried.

'Not yet.'

'Still you lock him away in a cell like some convicted evil-doer.'

'I would be heavily censured if he were allowed to return to the bush, out of official reach.'

'He came here of his own free will – '

'Because he's a Firbeck.' Edward picked his way round shards of jagged pottery. 'So arrogant he could not envisage his own implication in this case being taken seriously. Now he knows better. If he went away now, I doubt if we could rely on his showing up a second time.'

'You're treating him like a common criminal,' she persisted.

'I'm treating him as I would anybody else under serious suspicion.'

'He *is* my brother.'

'It is you who should be reminded of that, not I.'

Jassy stared at him, appalled. That mildness which had first drawn her to him was deceptive. Beneath it he was a mass of contradictory furies.

'Now I understand,' she said.

'He appears to think none of the decencies, none of the laws apply to him. He's gone too far.'

'Just because he loves me – '

'Because he's flogged a man to death.'

'A man who stole from him.' She nodded with distaste towards the barrack square outside. 'I've watched you flog many a man near to death for less. It was your job, you told me. Is *this* your job? Be honest with me: you haven't imprisoned Luke for murder, or attempted murder, or any such thing.'

Edward stood stiff and rather absurd in the middle of the small room. With terrible, steely honesty he said: 'Perhaps I have not. You could say that I have imprisoned him for theft rather than murder.'

'Theft?'

'He has stolen from me. My most treasured possession. If ever you were mine at all, which I wonder.'

She turned away from the stark anguish of his face.

'It's not my name you cry out in the night.' His voice cracked. 'Whose lips is it touch yours when we embrace? Mine? Whose arms encircle you when we are close?'

'Don't. Edward, I beg of you – '

'No, by God. Murder is nothing to what he has done to me.' Half blind with jealousy, he stumbled to the door. 'He has killed not just one man, but two – in different ways. Why should I lift a finger to make him comfortable?'

She heard the outer door slam, and a moment later saw her husband marching, with head and shoulders back, across the square. There was nothing to be hoped for from him. Jassy put her head against the cool glass of the window and strained to see some other promise, some ray of light on the frightening horizon.

Samuel paced up and down the veranda of the village store. It was impossible to stay still. He wanted to be doing something positive, getting his hands on the situation and tearing it open, settling it, going at it and conquering it by sheer physical force just as he had conquered so many a mile of forest clearance, ploughed up so many an acre of tough land. But there was nothing to be done: nothing but wait.

Anna Helmich edged demurely out of the store and stood by the rail as he stamped past, turned, and passed her again.

'I must go,' said Samuel.

'Where?'

'I don't know. I can't just stay here like this.'

'You must stay as long as you wish – or need.'

Her father had already made that generously clear. 'Stay as long as you have to,' he had said, and brooked no argument. 'We must show them, yes, how we all stand together? For myself I am glad if you stay a long time. But for your sake,' he had added gruffly, 'I hope it is short. So we say no more.'

It was hard to imagine this reserved, rather gauche man, with his passion for order and civility, having ever been married to the uproarious harridan in the tavern across the way. Yet they had lived together and, for some brief time, loved together – and had the attractive, fair-haired Anna to show for it.

Anna said gently: 'When will the doctor get here?'

It was the question that had been hammering in his mind, driving him up and down. Everything depended on what that doctor said. Why the devil wasn't he here: why couldn't he hurry?

Samuel shook his head.

'He'll tell us the man drowned.' She tried to soothe him. 'Luke will be free.'

The words were kindly but meaningless. Samuel stopped near the steps and glared down the unanswering street.

'Did you know,' he asked, 'that Luke was talking of going away?'

'No.' She sounded genuinely surprised.

'He wants to go farther out, start again. All at once, all in a great rush. I couldn't believe it. Can you imagine – after all we've been through. I wondered if, perhaps . . .'

He could not bear to go on.

'What?' Anna prompted.

'Don't you see, if he'd mentioned it some weeks ago, or any other time . . . before Nipper died . . . I wouldn't have this awful feeling that he's done something he has to run away from. Wouldn't he have told *you*?'

She shook her head. 'Why me?'

'Oh, I thought sometimes . . . wondered . . . I don't know.'

'What don't you know?'

'What there was between you.'

She laughed in soft wonderment. 'Samuel, you are just a little blind, I think.' There was a lilt in her tone he had never heard before. 'It is not Luke. It has never been Luke.'

Fleetingly his attention was distracted from the street and the barracks and the picture he kept building up of the doctor's arrival. Instead, there was a picture of a tall, sweet-mouthed girl with modestly questioning blue eyes, in a simple blue dress which clung to her body and moved as she moved, rose and fell with her quickened breathing, rustled as she put slender fingers up to pat her near-flaxen hair. A little blind? He had been more than that. She had managed to live unsullied in this grubby village, keeping herself – for whom? For a man with the sense to see her true and clear, and to treat her as she deserved.

But there was too much on his mind. This was not the

time. He saw the flicker of shy invitation in her eyes die away; but she smiled understandingly and said:

'Please, Samuel, you must eat something. You cannot trudge up and down all day and night. Come indoors. When there is news we shall know soon enough, never fear.'

He allowed himself to be coaxed to the table as the lamps were lit. They had scarcely begun to eat when they heard someone riding madly into the village from the west, pounding to a halt outside the tavern across the street. It could hardly be the doctor; but every fresh sound might mean something to Luke, to their whole situation. Samuel hurried out on to the veranda again, in time to see the rider slip from his horse and kick open the inn door.

'Fire!'

The door swung shut behind him.

Samuel, with Anna behind him, crossed the street and went into the bar.

Moll was slopping ale into tankards. 'If it comes here, lads, we'll drown it. Come on, m'dear, you look parched.'

The rider drank deeply and thankfully.

'Bottoms up,' yelled Moll.

Rosie, escaping from a customer's knee, looked worried. 'Fire?' Obviously the mere thought of it terrified her. She plucked at the newcomer's sleeve. 'How far away?'

'Thirty mile or so. You can see it from Miller's Pike. A big 'un.'

'London Bridge is burning down,' someone began to sing. 'Burning down . . .'

Samuel left Anna in the doorway, not venturing in as he strode to the counter.

Moll greeted him with unaffected warmth. 'How's your brother?'

'As well as you'd expect.'

'Come in for a noggin?'

'No, I – '

'You're always welcome.' She glanced past him at her daughter, and raised an inquisitive eyebrow.

Samuel said: 'Where's this fire, did you say?'

'West. Thirty miles, I'd say.' The rider sagged against the bar.

'Near Firbecks'?'

'Could be, aye. Yes, come to think on, that'd be about the direction.'

'Moll, I beg you – '

'Anything, Samuel,' she said archly.

'Get these men out of here. It'll take every one who can get there. My father's alone with Kate. And at a time like this, Luke . . . '

He left Moll to hector the men into leaving their drinks and setting out. It was a lot to ask – a crippling ride in the darkness, to face the most feared enemy in the country. But many of them had experienced that enemy before. They knew it had to be beaten – no matter how many times it came raging back, it had to be met and defeated. They were all together in this.

Samuel raced up the street to the barracks. There was nobody in Edward's quarters. He hurried round to the cell block, to find Edward sternly escorting Jassy away from an interview with Luke. Samuel blocked their way.

'There's an emergency. Edward, I implore you to release Luke. He'll return in time for your inquiry – that I'll vouch for.'

'May we take this a trifle more calmly?'

Samuel said: 'Fire. There's fire on our land. And only father and Kate there to fight it.'

There was a long shuddering moan from Luke's cell.

'Edward, you must,' said Jassy. 'Please. You *know* what it'll be like out there.'

The lieutenant's face was implacable. 'I know nothing.

All I have is an unconfirmed report of a fire which may be miles away, for all we know. If it has been caught in time, there's little likelihood of your father being in danger.'

'But how can you be sure of any such thing?' Samuel raged.

'I suggest you go and find out. There'll be plenty of volunteers to help if the emergency is genuine.'

'It's our home, Edward. Release Luke – God, if ever he was needed it's now. He'll come back afterwards. Put him on oath – put me on oath, anything . . . '

'Out of the question. A report has gone to Parramatta, and the doctor is on his way.'

'I give you my word.'

'Release one,' said Edward inflexibly, 'I'd have to release them all. I can make no exceptions, least of all on family grounds. Under no circumstances can I allow my personal feelings to interfere.'

'Your personal feelings?' said Jassy, amazed. 'Oh, I know them. You hypocrite.'

Samuel swung away out of the building and through the gates. There was no more time to waste. He heard the jingle of harness and saw a motley crowd of men and horses assembling outside *The Trooper's Rest.* He could only pray they were sober enough to last the journey, and strong enough to face whatever awaited them at its end.

The fire came blazing in from the far depths of the night, gobbling trees and scrub, sending greedy red tongues leaping into the sky. A blanket of smoke hung, folding and unfolding, along a five-mile front, thickening and then shredding at the mercy of the wind and the flames' fierce draught.

Kate tried to estimate the speed of the advance, and their own avenues of escape – if escape became inevitable.

'The sheep – where are they?'

'There's a thousand over Dragon's Rock,' said Morgan. 'A thousand on the ridge. And – '

'Get them down to the river. Keep them away from trees and dig away the grass round them, so there's nothing for the fire to burn.'

Morgan stared for a second or two, instinctively rebelling against her tone of authority. He knew where she came from, he didn't take orders from the likes of that. Then he said: 'Aye, missus.'

'Hurry. Both of you.'

Morgan and Shep hurried off.

Jason leaned despairingly on the veranda rail. 'We should get to the village.'

'I'm staying,' said Kate crisply.

'But what can we do?'

'For a start, we need wet cloths to beat out the flames.' She went indoors and began to pull down the window curtains. 'Fix them to poles. I'll fetch water.'

She balanced the yoke across her shoulders and lurched down to the stream. Her load was heavy, slowing her down, on the return climb. Smoke drifted over the ridge. It would not be long before flame broke through and started to encircle them. She bumped the buckets down close to Jason, who rolled lengths of curtain into the water.

Above the back of the house the hellish glow brightened in the sky.

'It'll go up like tinder,' Jason lamented. 'We should have built in stone.'

'Put your valuables in the saddlebags,' Kate ordered. 'Saddle the horses. And make sure they're securely tethered: they'll panic if the fire comes close.'

Jason nodded submissively, and hurried towards the stables.

Kate seized one of the improvised flails, and set off up the hill towards the swirling hot breath that puffed wickedly over the ridge. She heard a shout, and looked back. Six or seven horsemen were riding in past the barn. She stumbled her way back, and saw that the leader was Samuel.

'You're all right?' he called.

'So far.'

Quickly he appraised the work she had done, and waved to his father.

'We could see it as we rode down. All along the hill, and coming this way.' He looked around. 'Where are the sheep?'

'I set Morgan and Shep to drive them down to the river,' said Kate.

'Good.' He flashed her a quick appreciative smile. 'Did they round them all up in time?'

'No. There are still some on the ridge.'

'God, they'll be caught. That's the way it's coming.' He wheeled his horse, shouted orders at the men who had followed him. 'There're shovels in the barn. We'll need to dig a firebreak.'

Jason carried a saddlebag into the house and began to fill it.

Was this how it was all to end? All they had striven for, given their lives to, to be swept away in a cruel dream, reduced to ashes?

They worked on into the night, trying to keep to an orderly plan in the middle of confusion, shadows, smoke, and sudden alarms from one quarter or another. Morgan drove the last sheep down to their all too vulnerable haven by the water. Shep dug and scraped at the earth to create the only feeble defence they could trust. The men from the village flailed their way along the ridge, and gouged a long, wavering fire-break out of the ground, working in the teeth of the searing wind. Kate made tea and brought it to them; and stayed with them for a while, digging as feverishly as any of them. Then she went back to calm the horses, and to carry more water up the slope.

And it happened, as they had known it must. All at once the ragged, leaping flames had won the ridge and were poised to race down on the house.

Samuel raced along the edge of the fire-break, kicking shreds of grass away. Wherever a shower of sparks fell, one of the men would fall upon it with a flail. But the water was drying up, they could not drag buckets up fast enough, and the wall of flame was too long. If its ends should curl down too fast, they could all too easily out-flank the defenders.

Jason stood for a weary moment, near to collapse, in the shelter of the barn.

'Merciful God, Saviour of mankind, look with compassion upon thy children' – his voice was almost lost under the roar and crackle of the doomed hillside – 'destroy not their hopes, add not to their suffering . . . '

A great rain of sparks fell suddenly upon the roof of the barn, and it burst into flame.

Sparks were jumping the break now. Rivulets of fire ran behind the men's legs and danced skittishly towards the house. One of the horses began to scream in panic.

Jason and Samuel came together by the end of the house. Kate, her face blackened and her bare arms covered with scratches, blundered close and almost fell against Samuel. She was at the end of her tether.

'Come back!' Samuel yelled at the flailing, unyielding men. 'It's behind you – get clear!'

Flaring tufts of grass were kicked up as the men finally abandoned their last-ditch defence.

'What can we do?' panted Jason.

'We must get the horses away.' Samuel looked up at the blazing roof of the barn. 'I think it's the end.'

Dr Harty was a lank, stooping man with an ancient top-hat as pockmarked as his features. As he descended from the trap which had brought him here at this unreasonable midmorning hour, he glanced longingly at the façade of *The Trooper's Rest.*

Moll bounded out on to the veranda, tugging her bodice into the nearest approach to decency it was capable of achieving.

'Doctor?'

'Harty, ma'am. Hale and hearty, they used to say. Though damn me if time hasn't made a lie of it. I'd be on the right road for the barracks?'

'Near, yes, near. But not so near a quart of ale would come amiss.'

Harty blinked, and scratched his scrawny chin. 'Ah, you're right. What it is to find a woman who understands.'

Moll led him inside. 'You don't remember me, do you?'

The doctor looked her up and down. 'I'll be bound, ma'am, there are some parts strike me familiar.' He screwed up his eyes in the shadows of the tap-room. 'Though it's not a fact I could put a name to.'

'The Sidney Tavern?' said Moll. 'Flinders Street.'

'Why, bless my soul. Molly, is it?'

'It is indeed.'

'What times we had!'

Harty was delighted. He was even more delighted when Moll poured a brimming mug and pushed it towards him.

Rosie came in, keeping back until Moll gave some sign of encouraging her or waving her out again.

'And my poor little daughter!' said Moll loudly. She put out an arm towards Rosie. 'See the doctor's well supplied, my dear. Reach him down a noggin of the strong stuff – ah, of course you will, Doctor, it's good for the damp and the ache in the bones – pour it, dearie, afore you tell him the troubles that blight your life.'

Dr Harty sank into a chair. He drank with noisy relish, but the gaze he cast on Rosie was shrewd enough.

'She don't look blighted to me.'

'You should see her chest. Pains her awful.' Moll stood for a moment between Rosie and the doctor. 'Tell him,' she said with mournful clarity, 'what Nipper done to you afore he went and drownded hisself.'

Rosie went to the counter and returned with a glass of golden liquor to set beside the mug of ale.

'Drowned?' said Harty.

'Aye, like sorrows. Bottoms up, Doctor.' Moll eyed Rosie over the top of her mug. 'Be brave a little longer, child, till the doctor gets a proper look at you. Come on, let's have two more' – she sank into the chair beside Harty's – 'while poor little Rosie tells you about Nipper.'

Luke stood by the bars looking down the corridor as Edward Elliott opened the door of the room where Nipper Clarke had been lying. The doctor came out, leaned against the wall, and belched.

'Well?' said Edward impatiently.

'Drowned,' said Dr Harty.

'You're quite certain?'

'Like a sorrow. Bottoms up.'

The lieutenant stood rigid for a moment, then pulled himself together and walked towards Luke's cell. For an instant he stopped, glancing back at his sergeant.

'See the drunken fool signs a report.'

'Now see here, sir, if you think a pr'f'ssional man like myself . . . hic . . . if you think I'll stand for that kind of . . . '

Edward reached the bars of the cell. Luke was waiting for him.

Edward said: 'I'm letting you go.'

'You don't have much choice, do you?' There was no triumph in Luke's voice: simply an abysmal weariness.

'You're to leave us alone. D'you hear?'

A trooper came with keys and unfastened the door. Edward waved him away.

Luke stepped out. 'Be kind to Jassy,' he said, 'or you won't be left alone. I'll kill you.'

'You're quite capable of it.'

'Yes.'

Edward waved along the corridor to the outer door and freedom.

'You've been lucky. You may not be so lucky again.'

He escorted Luke stiffly to the outside world.

'So Nipper was drowned,' said Luke.

'According to that drunken doctor, yes.'

'And you don't want to believe it.'

'Should I?'

Luke left him. As he was about to ride away, he was gripped by an impulse to ride across the square, to the lieutenant's quarters, to see Jassy once more and tell her . . .

But what was there left to tell?

He had a vision of flames engulfing the homestead, and of his father and Samuel going down before a tidal wave of fire. There was only one place for him now. He galloped down the street, and on beyond the boundaries and on, until he saw wisps of smoke like cloud streamers against the sky, and urged the horse on.

He was too late, much too late. That he saw as he came over the last hill. The pastures below were blackened. Smoke drifted still from the wide basin of some awful, natural fireplace. The hill behind him was still green: ahead the folds of rising land were no more than charred carcases.

And yet in one corner, set against the blackest of slopes, there was still a patch of green. The barn was a gutted ruin. But the house was still, incredibly, there.

He rode down, and a man he recalled having once seen in the village straightened an aching back, called a welcome, and went back to flailing a smouldering patch of grass. Two others were mechanically plodding to and fro with buckets of water.

The fences of the paddocks were damaged – whole lengths burnt away, leaving raw ends and crumbling mounds of ash. A couple of bullocks wandered about in a daze, uncontrolled but doing no apparent harm. And up the slope from the river came Morgan and Shep, slowly driving the sheep back.

Kate was first to see Luke. She had been carrying a pail, but dropped it, and ran to catch his horse's bridle.

'You've come,' she cried. 'You're back.' She looked even more beaten and bedraggled than when she had first come to the homestead. Yet also, in some way he could not explain, she was beautiful – and fulfilled.

'Too late to be of any use, it seems,' he said wryly.

Jason and Samuel were hurrying towards him.

'They have set you free.'

'You . . . have to go back?' said Samuel.

'No, I don't have to go back.'

'God is merciful,' said Jason.

Suddenly they were all talking at once. And over and over again it was Kate's name on the men's lips – the story of how Kate had organized the men before Samuel returned, how she had been behind Samuel and beside him, and how she had protected first one side of the danger area and then another.

Luke stared at her, and she stared unflinchingly back at him.

'You?' he said quietly. 'You did all that?'

'We did what was possible,' she said. 'It was not enough.'

'But the house – '

'When all seemed lost,' said Jason, 'the wind veered. My prayers were answered.'

Luke walked towards the front door, smoke-stained but unharmed. He found that he had taken Kate's hand in his. It was harsh and cracked, skin roughened and nails broken in the unremitting hours of battle which lay behind her. He wanted to tell her that it would not always be like this, must not be – there had to be a life worthy of her, not too far into the future.

'Next time we shall build in stone.' Jason was walking behind them. 'Perhaps higher up. A fine stone house.'

Luke raised his eyes to the charred ridge, and knew there were still green hills beyond, and beyond that again.

'So the imperfections of time and place shall pass you by.'

'In stone,' Jason rhapsodized, 'and larger. Much larger, so that you can rear your families and keep them about us. Time you started, both of you. And we will stand together. If we are to fight this place we must stand as one.'

Luke drew Kate to one side and let his father lead the way back into their home.

At his elbow, Samuel said: 'You can't leave him, Luke. You can't take him on into another wilderness – and you can't go alone, and leave him here.'

Jason turned in the doorway and waited for them.

Not knowing what to say, or what he might want to say tomorrow or in the gruelling weeks which lay ahead, Luke shook his head.

'The men need rest,' said Samuel. 'Without them, we'd have been lost. And when they've rested, I'll take them back to the village and see they lack for nothing.'

'And stay with Anna?' said Luke.

'With Anna's father.'

The two brothers smiled a slow, companionable smile.

Luke said: 'And thank her mother for me.'

'Yes, without Moll whipping those men out here for us – '

'I meant more than that.'

'Oh?'

'She'll know,' said Luke.

'Luke. About that business – about Nipper – '

'I'm here!' Luke silenced him with a roar. 'Isn't that enough? We've got to survive. The only way we can.' He turned to Kate, who had shuddered once at the sudden bellow of his voice, but was immediately calm again. He said, straight at her: 'Did I kill Nipper?'

'No,' she said simply.

He broke away and walked towards the skeleton of the crumpled barn. When he rested his hand on a blackened beam, the blackness smeared away on to his palm.

Kate came after him: not in pursuit, but as if there were nothing else she could do.

He watched Samuel go into the house with their father. When he and Kate were truly alone together, he said:

'If I must stay here, as Samuel says I must, I . . . I can't face it alone. Not any more.'

'You won't be alone. Your family – '

'Not enough,' he said. He closed his eyes, exhausted. 'Kate, I'm no catch. I'm not kind, I can never be restful, I'll forever be a scourge to anyone close to me. One day, when all this work has been done over again, I shall want to be free and move on again. All this I know. It is nothing to offer a woman, is it?'

Her hand was in his again. 'Are you offering it?' she said.

'Kate, be with me.'

'I'll be with you.'

He sighed, as an intolerable burden was eased from him. When he opened his eyes again he looked long at Kate, then beyond her, and said:

'And now . . . there is work to do.'